With her sophisticated looks, fiery and expressive eyes, strong personality and bearing, Suchitra Sen was an instant hit with the youth of Bengal from the 1950s through the 1970s. Uttam Kumar, with his famous smile and charming demeanour, too was a phenomenon to reckon with. And together, they were an unbeatable romantic pair. Of the 60 films Suchitra Sen worked in, 30 were with Uttam Kumar. The duo gave a string of hits such as *Sagarika* (1956), *Harano Sur* (1957), *Indrani* (1958), *Agnipariksha* (1954), *Saptapadi, Grihadaha* (1967), all part of Bengali cinematic history today. Interestingly, these films are remembered not only as the best of Uttam and Suchitra, but as cinema that is poignant, sensitive and heart-rending.

The star pair ushered in what came to be known as the golden era of Bengali cinema. A whole generation of men and women, especially from the 1950s to the 1970s, grew up on the Uttam and Suchitra magic. Coupled with astounding music and great scripts, Uttam and Suchitra starrers became simply unbeatable.

Uttam Kumar and Suchitra Sen: Bengali Cinema's First Couple is a tribute to this unparalleled star-duo of Bengali cinema.

Maitreyee B Chowdhury is a web columnist and creative writer, and writes on cinema and social issues. She is the author of *Reflections on My India,* a book on Indian traditions and spirituality. Maitreyee is featured amongst other Indian writers such as Gulzar, Shahashi Tharoor and Deepti Naval in an anthology of Indian writers *Celebrating India.*

Uttam Kumar and Suchitra Sen
Bengali Cinema's First Couple

Maitreyee B Chowdhury

OM
Om Books International

First published in 2013 by

OM

Om Books International

Corporate & Editorial Office
A-12, Sector 64, Noida 201 301
Uttar Pradesh, India
Phone: +91 120 477 4100
Email: editorial@ombooks.com
Website: www.ombooksinternational.com

Sales Office
4379/4B, Prakash House, Ansari Road
Darya Ganj, New Delhi 110 002, India
Phone: +91 11 2326 3363, 2326 5303
Fax: +91 11 2327 8091
Email: sales@ombooks.com
Website: www.ombooks.com

ISBN: 978-81-87108-56-6

Printed in India

10 9 8 7 6 5 4 3 2 1

Contents

Melody Regained

Uttam Kumar and Suchitra Sen

It is late in the evening. Dark clouds gather in the sky. Tiny flowers cling tenaciously to gently swaying branches. Windswept and romantic, a man and a woman slowly come alive under a tree. The black-and-white frames capture the love-glazed, half-closed eyes of the man, resting his head on the lap of the woman. Both wear delicate garlands, and in a haunting voice, she sings *'Tumi Je Amar, Ogo Tumi Je Amar...'*

One of the most romantic scenes from an Uttam Kumar-Suchitra Sen starrer, *Harano Sur* (1957) takes us down memory lane to an era of romance and beauty, captured forever on celluloid!

What began as a fascination—watching this couple's films over and over again—inspired *Uttam Kumar and Suchitra Sen: Bengali Cinema's First Couple.* Several literary pieces have been written about Uttam and Suchitra, yet the thirst to know more about Bengali cinema's legendary romantic pair remains unquenchable. This book is not only a tribute to Uttam and Suchitra but also an effort to understand what made Uttam and Suchitra steal their way into the hearts of millions of fans the world over.

Bengal has undeniably produced many great names in the field of acting and entertainment, some far more talented than the duo. Yet time has not worn down the memory of this pair. Uttam and Suchitra ushered in a new age of star-power and charisma. The why's and how's of their togetherness mystified an entire generation who took the pairing for granted. For these cinegoers, Uttam and Suchitra were not just cultural icons but champions of romance and ageless love. They were the reason many watched Bengali movies. For a generation of cinephiles, both regional and national, Uttam and Suchitra were truly an unbeatable pair!

And they continue to mesmerise the younger crop of successful directors and actors in Bengal, and beyond, with their magic.

1

Two Stars are Born

Days and nights pass and ages bloom and fade like flowers.
Thou knowest how to wait.
Thy centuries follow each other perfecting a small wild flower.

Rabindranath Tagore

In Bengali cinema, few screen couples have generated as much interest as the charming Uttam Kumar and the beautiful Suchitra Sen. What made these stars larger-than-life is a question that foxes many. The phenomenal rise of the two as stars rather than as actors may be attributed to several factors.

Any mention of early Bengali cinema immediately evokes memories of remarkable plots that were a delight to watch. Cinema then was primarily about a story that touched the heart, its appeal and beauty stemming from cultural rootedness. Often cinema was a piece of literature in motion. Even those who found reading Sharat Chandra Chattopadhyay, Bibhutibhushan Bandopadhyay, or Bankim Chandra Chattopadhyay difficult, appreciated watching films based on their works.

Bengali cinema of the forties was renowned for its romance and aesthetics. It received international recognition primarily because it was inspired by the love of cinema and not necessarily by commercial considerations. Post-Independence Bengali cinema was evidently educative and realistic, and at times, patriotic as well.

Tollygunge, in South Kolkata, was the hub of the Bengali film industry, the grooming ground for the artistically inclined cinema anchored in elitist sentiments that gave us landmark films like Debaki Bose's *Chandidas* (1932) and PC Barua's *Devdas* (1935). Much credit for this actually goes to a film-loving public, educated and aware as they were of the classics, and contemporary literary movements.

The media, too, actively promoted and advocated such cinema. The habit of reading film journals helped cinephiles develop a taste for good cinema, and polish their understanding and theory of cinema, and its versatility as a serious medium of expression. The public was intelligent enough to pick out new thought patterns that broke away from traditions and 'methods' to venture, beyond, into the 'madness' of what cinema is all about.

Classics, such as *Kabuliwala* (1956), *Devdas, Meghe Dhaka Tara* (1960) were also extremely popular those days. Pioneers like Satyajit Ray, Ritwik Ghatak, Mrinal Sen and Bimal Roy provided direction to Bengali cinema by fostering a great film culture not only among the intelligentsia within India, but abroad, too, where their films received much critical acclaim.

Kolkata of yore also boasted of several film theatres, especially New Theatre. The role of these theatres in producing some of the finest technicians, actors and directors in the country to date, can hardly be ignored. Cornwallis (later renamed Shree), Picture Palace (later renamed Elite) and Rupbani were part of that history.

At the same time, theatres, such as Metro, Globe, and New Empire regularly showed Hollywood, European and American parallel cinema.

Exposed to great home-grown cinema, film clubs, which also published magazines of high standard with articles on world cinema, mushroomed. Magazines, such as *Prasad*, *Chitrabani*, and *Rupanjali* were more like documentaries on both regional and world cinema.

Given this background, one would have thought that Bengali cinema would have been a great money-spinner. Strangely, such was not the case. Its lacklustre performance at the box office has been attributed to mounting comparisons with Bollywood and its glamour.

Bengali cinema needed rejuvenation, after the 1950s—less in terms of scripts, acting or technicians, and more in areas of presentation of a cinema and star-power. It needed to be less elitist, with greater mass appeal.

Young Bengalis of this time craved for something different from the regular village-based scripts with their repetitive settings and treatment. Their prayers found an answer in this young and good-looking couple who scorched the Bengali screen from the 1950s to the 1970s, not only with their acting but also with their screen presence. In an era starved of poetic romance, Bengali cinema desperately clung on to this pair.

From their very first film, *Sare Chuattor* (1953), their romance and personalities ushered in one of the most glorious periods of Bengali cinema, in terms of both popularity and box-office gains. Though Uttam-Suchitra evoked tenderness and sensuality, the pair acted in several serious films, too, with a social message.

Gopal Krishna Roy, a friend of Suchitra, says, ‘As a romantic pair, they were simply superb. While there are many artistes who can show a love affair on-screen, what Uttam and Suchitra projected was beyond a normal love affair. It was a sort of meeting of two perfect souls who not only complemented each other physically, but also shared a strong platonic bond. Their emotional-spiritual bond made the pairing so special.'

This was also the era when melodrama overtook intense realism in Bengali cinema. The remarkable change in audience sensibilities was evident when they welcomed the romantic opulence and escapades presented by Uttam and Suchitra, at times urban adventures tracing journeys from the country to the city, and the consequent psychological and emotional changes.

A plausible reason for the success of this pair was that romance as portrayed by Uttam and Suchitra had hardly been explored in Bengali cinema earlier. In addition, their films largely traded the backdrop of rural rusticity for that of the slick city, depicting a lifestyle and glamour that had not been shown earlier. Romance, instead of scenes weighed down with sorrow, trials and tribulations, ushered in a breath of fresh air. The Bengali youth readily identified with the star pair's on-screen longing for each other, their intense looks, and even the rebellious streak they exhibited.

The myriad backdrops used in the films added to the appeal of the stories. In *Saptapadi* (1961), the turmoil and rage within were carried forward with the story to remote corners of Bengal scarred by the trauma of war. On the other hand, *Sare Chuattor* had the youth-friendly atmosphere of a boarding-house full of boys and their delirious antics; *Harano Sur* explored an entirely different world of partial memory loss.

Uttam and Suchitra's entry into Bengali cinema could not have been better timed. While Bengali cinema had highly creative minds, great technicians and wonderful stories to tell, it lacked glamour and stardom. Suchitra, with her sophisticated looks and mannerisms, was like no other heroine of her age. Her fiery and expressive eyes, her strong personality and bearing made her an instant hit with the Bengali youth. With his famous smile and charming demeanour, Uttam, too, was a phenomenon to reckon with. Suchitra, the glamorous diva, sported and basked in her 'Mrs Sen' air. As for Uttam, Satyajit Ray described him as a person, 'every mother wanted as a son, every sister wanted as a brother, and every girl wanted as a lover.'

Neither Uttam nor Suchitra needed the other to stand out. Yet together, they made an unbeatable pair, a verity borne out by the box-office collections: of the 60 films Suchitra worked in, 30 were with Uttam. The duo gave a string of hits, such as *Harano Sur, Agnipariksha* (1954), *Sagarika* (1956), *Indrani* (1958), *Saptapadi, Grihadaha* (1967), all part of Bengal's cinema history today. Interestingly, these films are remembered not only as the best of Uttam and Suchitra, but as cinema that was poignant and sensitive.

The tremendous success of Uttam and Suchitra encouraged many to exploit their chemistry. In a bid to cash in on their appeal, directors and producers sought the same expressions and styles of their hit films, little realising that good cinema is not about just good acting, but a blend of several other factors. As a consequence, some of their films seemed repetitive and did not measure up to the quality their pairing was associated with.

Uttam and Suchitra ushered in the golden era of Bengali cinema. A whole generation of men and women, especially from the 1950s to the 1970s, flocked to cinema halls to watch films that they could relate to with characters they could idolise. Backed with marvellous music and great scripts, Uttam and Suchitra starrers simply stole the thunder.

In the words of actress Madhabi Mukherjee, a famous contemporary, the two were like 'Radha-Krishna on the silver screen.'

2

The Rise of Popular Bengali Cinema

The crowds of flowers come out of a sudden,
From nobody knows where,
And dance upon the grass in wild glee.

Rabindranath Tagore

Popular Bengali cinema of this time, notwithstanding its intellectual limitations, made great strides. Thanks to a pair like Uttam and Suchitra, cinema became both profitable and entertaining. Ritwik Ghatak, Satyajit Ray and Mrinal Sen admirers may strongly disagree and consider mainstream films rather pedestrian compared to the serious realistic films made by these stalwarts. However, cinema being a medium of the masses, the masses of this era had expressed their mandate.

Uttam was certainly a name to contend with, not so much for his contribution to serious cinema (he worked with Satyajit Ray), but primarily because of his mass appeal. Even Suchitra, who was not particularly interested in serious cinema and is known to have turned down an opportunity of working with Satyajit Ray, commanded a massive fan following.

Many say that Uttam and Suchitra would have never been remembered but for their on-screen romances. This, however, may not be entirely true. Romance being an essential part of life and something to cherish, they certainly made their mark as a romantic duo. But Uttam and Suchitra contributed their share to realistic cinema as well. In fact, the cult status that Uttam and Suchitra enjoyed made it easier for them to initiate changes, set new trends and introduce new concepts that were quickly absorbed by society.

When Suchitra donned the hat of a professional woman, she lent to it a lot of glamour, making women all over Bengal want to emulate her. Similarly, people identified with Uttam far more than they did with a symbolic abstract character portrayed in parallel cinema.

Ever since the 'bioscope' days of the 1890s, Bengali cinema's relationship with the audience had been somewhat turbulent. Bengali films, like other regional films, originated from theatre and witnessed the emergence of different genres of cinema over a period of time. In fact, the experiments conducted in Bengali cinema during this phase remain unparalleled in India cinema of those times.

Popular literary works formed a solid base for Bengali cinema. In the early stages, Bengali cinema was not categorised into realistic cinema and popular cinema. Be it *Billwamangal* (1919), *Bilat Ferat* (1921), or *Jamai Shashthi* (1931), early Bengali films were driven by the need to express emotions on celluloid. These films generated a keen interest in cinema among the Bengalis of that era. Bengali cinema already had brilliant actors, technicians and directors even at that time, and did not indulge in extreme realism or intellectualism. Their fascination for the medium combined with the desire to showcase good cinema that would be widely appreciated.

Films of two famous Bengali heroes of the 1930s—Debaki Bose and PC Barua—enjoyed rare popularity. Later, both Barua and Bose directed many films which gave a new direction to Bengali cinema. Their films were as popular with the masses as with the intellectuals. The divide between popular cinema and intellectual cinema was further blurred by directors, such as Bimal Roy and actors like Kanan Devi and Pahari Sanyal, who carried off both such roles with equal ease.

The 'Parallel Cinema' movement, which began in the 1950s, was pioneered mainly by Ritwik Ghatak, Satyajit Ray and Mrinal Sen. Strangely; this period coincided with the emergence of Uttam in films, such as *Basu Paribar* (1952) and the iconic pairing of Uttam and Suchitra in *Sare Chuattor.*

In its attempt to capture the essence of Bengali society, realistic cinema of that time explored drought-stricken fields, and life in shanties—a limited representation of a culture otherwise steeped in literature, music and dance. Blending both kinds of cinema depicting a society that was as much artistically inclined as it was poverty-stricken was a more balanced projection of reality, something that popular Bengali cinema set out to do. *Shilpi* (1956), an Uttam and Suchitra starrer, was a bold step in this direction. With the release of *Agnipariksha,* popular Bengali cinema engendered even more openness, realism, and introspection. The audience responded heartily.

Popular cinema, especially from the 1950s to the 1970s, had beautifully designed sets and relatively striking camera movements. Equal emphasis was laid on the accompanying razzmatazz of farcical and song-and-dance routines.

However, neo-realism and intellectual cinema could not sustain the industry. Though parallel cinema brought much critical acclaim to Bengal, there was enough space for *Pather Panchali* (1955) and *Agnipariksha* to co-exist. If the common man sought an alternative to realistic cinema in the form of something that was more youthful and vibrant, Uttam-Suchitra starrers provided the answer.

Popular Bengali cinema, especially Uttam and Suchitra starrers, represented the same culture and society that parallel cinema did. However, the themes being emotional and melodramatic helped viewers escape from the quotidian drudgery to a world closer to his dreams, even if unattainable.

Interestingly, this phase coincided with the emergence of glamorous Hindi films in a big way and their impact on the Bengali audience—they were wooed away from regional cinema. Large amounts of money were offered for the monopoly rights to show popular Hindi films in theatres.

At this juncture, the arrival of filmmakers, such as Asit Sen and Nirmal Dey was a boon to Bengali cinema. Theirs was a fresh cinema that bordered on the contemporary—an effective fusion of realism and popular song-and-dance culture. Directors, such as Bimal Roy, Nabyendu Chatterjee, Tapan Sinha, Sukhen Das and Anjan Chowdhury made films that had attractive commercial ingredients—interesting character portrayals, and thematic and technical novelty. These films slowly won back the Bengali audience to home-grown Bengali fare.

At this critical juncture in Bengali cinema, two youthful faces brought with them the promise of a new dawn. Uttam and Suchitra showcased the fusion of sensible cinema and popular entertainment, with good stories, pleasant music, youthful vigour, and a dash of the much-needed romance.

During this period, the inclusion of melodrama as well as song and dance found several takers even though intellectuals stridently dismissed them as 'not-classy'. Amusingly, actress and director Aparna Sen, observes, 'We were not allowed to see populist Bengali films like *Harano Sur, Sagarika,* etc. Suchitra-Uttam starrers were a big no-no. *Pather Panchali* was the very first Bengali film I saw. It is a living irony that later I became a leading star in those very populist films I was not allowed to watch earlier.'

Whatever be the prejudices against popular cinema, audience who did not relate to the revolutionary parallel cinema movement, more than welcomed the new couple on the block. Be it for their glamour or their magnetic pairing, Uttam and Suchitra wove romance into the Bengali psyche through popular cinema.

Makers of parallel cinema have often been accused of being elitist, catering more to an international audience, than on home turf. Glimpses of Italian Neo-Realism often clashed with the traditional mould of Indian cinema in the works of stalwarts, such as Satyajit Ray, Ritwik Ghatak and Mrinal Sen. In fact, Satyajit Ray often spoke of the influence of the Western way of filmmaking on his work. The themes of these films mostly revolved around economic injustice against the powerless, uprooting of people from their homes and the consequent bereavement and loss of social status. Examples, such as *Nagarik* (completed in 1952), *Meghe Dhaka Tara* and *Padatik* (1973) were loud, as much in content as in other aspects, such as the use of sound and editing style—a determined effort to shake the audience out of its complacency.

While Bengalis did not question the greatness of this genre of cinema, and it remained intellectually stimulating, it was the Uttam and Suchitra melodramatic romances they could readily identify with. Uttam was the dream hero, the everyday man and a flamboyant star, rolled into one. To add to this allure, adaptations from Bengali literary classics ensured that the scripts never faltered. The popularity of film music composed by stalwarts of the time made the journey pleasantly melodious, too.

Most popular Bengali films were also social dramas mirroring contemporary society. They dealt with issues, such as exploitation by zamindars, class divide, Westernisation of the Kolkata elte, impact of religion, customs and rituals prevalent in rural Bengal, and more. However, unlike parallel cinema, these issues blended well with the storyline in popular cinema. Despite being vastly entertaining, they sent home some important messages.

Bengali cinema boasted of quite a few good character-actors including Pahari Sanyal, Dhiraj Bannerji, Chhabi Biswas, Sadhya Bannerjee and Molina Devi. Despite their great acting skills, none of them were stars in the true sense of the term. Uttam and Suchitra films on the other hand were sentimental sojourns. *Shilpi*, for instance, was a tear-jerker replete with drama, and therefore, a cathartic experience for its viewers.

The juxtaposition of melodrama and scintillating songs, picturised on Uttam and Suchitra added an edge to their fims. Audience young and old fell head over heels in love with Uttam and Suchitra, and their films. Most producers cashed in on this popularity, with films running to packed houses on all shows.

Uttam and Suchitra explored the various ups and downs of life while upholding righteousness, a major reason behind the astonishing success of a pair. Suchitra highlighted the plight of women of that age. With interesting and unusual storylines and author-backed roles, Uttam and Suchitra had audience glued to their seats. Apart from the customary melodrama, the pair also acted in films based on novels by Sharat Chandra Chattopadhyaya, such as *Rajlakshmi O Srikanto* (1958) and *Kamallata* (1969).

Agnipariksha ushered in a spate of commercial successes in the Bengali film industry. Its well-deserved acclaim was evident in the love that the audience showered on the golden duo. After this film, Uttam and Suchitra as a pair never looked back and successfully fuelled the dreams of thousands of young men and women who not only identified with them, but also saw them mirroring their own aspirations.

Of course, over time, Uttam and Suchitra matured into fine actors. The overtly romantic and loud drama soon gave way to fine and well-restrained performances. They soon rose above the tag of 'method actors' and established their credibility. An analysis of their acting capabilities—either individually or together—in early films, such as *Sare Chuattor* or *Shilpi* shows lack of sophistication. The loudness of these films made way for the more refined performances in films, such as *Saptapadi*, *Har Mana Har* (1972), *Harano Sur* and *Kamallata*.

Insiders credit the revival of the Bengali film industry of that period to the tremendous popularity of the star duo, and to the one-man phenomenon called Uttam. Satyajit Ray chose Uttam for *Nayak* (1966) and *Chiriyakhana* (1967). Despite Uttam's tremendous fan following, Ray faced a lot of flak for his choice from some quarters. Yet, success of these films was finally an acknowledgment of Uttam's talent.

The perception that artistic cinema was good cinema, and popular cinema was cheap was laid to rest by Uttam and Suchitra. Their choice of films convinced the audience and even the fence-sitters that they were more than pretty faces.

With Uttam and Suchitra, an entire generation of lovers sang *'Ei Poth Jodi Na Shesh Hoy...'* A romantic and happy ending had the audience believe that ultimately things would be fine in a life otherwise wrought with challenges.

Uttam and Suchitra starrers also showcased glamour like never before. Unlike realistic cinema, in which viewers never got a chance to fantasise about a star or a situation, Uttam and Suchitra starrers offered much to dream about. The Bengali audience found their very own matinee idols who spoke a language that was their own, and still remained a notch above their regular lives. The windswept scenes, Sucitra in colourful nylon sarees, the actors in soft focus and the beautifully done-up sets, all culminated in a dream-fantasy that the viewer would take home to re-live and dream about at leisure. Uttam and Suchitra's sublime and poetic screen romance, made them local demi-gods.

The emergence of private producers, in contrast to the semi-government aided parallel films, effected a change of scene, ushering in sensible commercial cinema. These producers also lend credence to the star-value system as they believed that the success of a film largely depended on the stars. Pure popular cinema gave viewers exactly what they wanted: big stars, costumes, dubbed acting, detailed sets, delightful visuals, technical extravaganza, and innovative portrayal of love in all its forms. Romance, poetry, man-woman relationships, family politics, and popular sentiments—all came together on celluloid in varied proportions, invading the Bengali cinegoers' sensibilities. The audience lapped it all up.

It is noteworthy, however, that even while depicting popular culture, Bengali cinema from the 1950s to the 1970s remained intrinsically 'Bengali' in nature.

Songs by Geeta Dutt, Sandhya Mukhopadhay, Asha Bhonsle, Hemanta Kumar Mukhopadhay and Manna Dey, among others, greatly contributed to the success of many Uttam and Suchitra films. Enchanting and evergreen compositions, such as '*Tumi Je Amar*', '*Ei Poth Jodi Na Shesh Hoy*', '*Nir Chhoto Khoti Nei*' and '*Shuno Bondhu*' linger in the memory of generations of cinephiles who even today associate Uttam and Suchitra films with such classic compositions.

There was plenty of scope for experimentation and filmmakers, including Tapan Sinha, Ajoy Kar, Asit Sen, and Tarun Majumdar gave popular Bengali cinema a distinct identity. After watching films like *Harano Sur*, *Deep Jweley Jai* (1959), *Saptapadi, Saat Pake Bandha* (1963) and *Uttar Falguni* (1963), one can't help but admire the quality of their content, technical expertise and aesthetics. They definitely matched the best of Hindi cinema of the time.

It was probably a coming together of various factors that made popular Bengali cinema earn the respect of critics. A wide choice of subjects, masterful use of Bengali literature in cinematic adaptations, mature storytelling with visual appeal, clearly gave a new genre of films which may not always have portrayed the intense realism of the parallel cinema Bengalis were used to, but it ranked highly among good cinema. The long queue of filmgoers in front of theatres, braving odds to catch the first show, especially of the Uttam and Suchitra starrers, was evidence enough of their popularity with the *hoi polloi.*

3

The Stars and the Persons

In many a morning and eve thy footsteps have been heard
And thy messenger has come within my heart and called me in secret.
I know not only why today my life is all astir,
And a feeling of tremulous joy is passing through my heart.

Rabindranath Tagore

Suchitra Sen evokes the image of a woman of incredible beauty and grace, with large haunting eyes. Yet she remains an enigma. While her acting skills had worthy equals, none came close to her 'star' personality. Be it her carriage, demeanour, attitude towards life, or even her sudden retirement and withdrawal from public life, Suchitra remains a mystery. A look at Suchitra's life and films reveals an intelligent woman intensely aware of her capabilities and charisma, and who went to great length to retain her mystique. A veteran of 60 films, she lent her inherent charm and poise to each character she portrayed. She mesmerised not only men, but an entire generation of women, too. They imitated her personality, carriage, smile, and even dressed like her in Bengal and beyond. During Durga Puja celebrations, idols of Lakshmi and Saraswati (Goddesses of Wealth and Learning, respectively) were known to have been modelled on her face. Such was the adulation she received in Bengal.

Much like today, her early life remains shrouded in mystery. She was born on 6th April 1931 (the year is still debated), to Karunamoy Dasgupta and Indira Devi in a small town called Pabna, now in Bangladesh. Her father was the headmaster of a school in Pabna. Suchitra's real name was Roma and she belonged to a large family of three brothers, an elder sister named Uma, and three younger sisters Hena, Leena, and Runa. The family was steeped in music and dance, and remembered as polite and amicable.

Roma was a beauty. The best looking of the sisters, she went to school in a white sari with a red border. A girl with an enchanting smile, she made friends easily. Friends like Fulrani Chowdhury (later Kanjilal) affirmed that Roma participated in all cultural activities in Pabna Girls High School. Despite being an average student, Roma had a certain air about her. The way she wore her sarees or the way she walked, set her apart in a crowd.

After Partition, her family relocated to West Bengal. Soon thereafter, the young Roma was married to Dibanath Sen, the son of a wealthy industrialist in Bengal. It is believed that no dowry was demanded for Roma at a time when the practice was rampant.

Roma took on the role of the lady-of-the-house. Conscious of her role as the daughter-in-law of a prestigious family, she conducted herself accordingly. This may have been the reason she remained so unapproachable on the sets of her films.

Interestingly, Roma had initially set her sight on a singing career. During a visit to a recording studio in Park Street with her husband, she was offered her first role in a Sukumar Dasgupta film. She was christened Suchitra by Nitish Roy, an assistant of Dasgupta. Though her ambition of making it big as a singer never really materialised, much later in life, she did sing for Kamal Ghosh's Megaphone. The lyrics were written by her favourite lyricist Gauri Prasanna Majumdar, while Barin Chattopadhyay was the music composer.

Suchitra's journey into the world of Bengali cinema was not a smooth one. Besides fighting her way up through several screen tests and meetings with directors, she also encountered formidable resistance at home—her responsibilities as the daughter-in-law and a mother to a daughter, and her father-in-law's opinion about working women. Later, the family, especially her husband, supported her and even tried the Bimal Roy-connection (her mother-in-law's brother), to get her a foothold in Bengali cinema.

'Mrs Sen', as she came to be known in the Bengali film circle, was probably the first Indian actress to enter films as a young mother. Today, she is the forerunner of three generations of actors, including her daughter, Moon Moon Sen, and her granddaughters, Raima and Riya, who bear the famous 'Sen' surname.

With her beauty and grace alone Suchitra made an impact on the audience from the very first film. Her family's affluence only added to her appeal at a time when most actors were compelled to work for a living. To the amazement and curiosity of the audience, Suchitra's films showcased a woman much ahead of her times, often playing the role of professionals—a doctor in *Harano Sur*, a nurse in *Saptapadi* or an artist in *Jiban Trishna* (1957). In every way, she stood out, successfully carving a niche for herself rather early in her career.

The way she dressed, her makeup, her way of talking, everything bespoke of a woman in command of herself and accustomed to attention. Her awareness of her social status added to her charisma. Her fashion sense was well ahead of her times, too, especially in Bengal. The way she wore her sarees, her elaborate hair do's or her sunglasses became a rage among the youth.

Dhiren Deb, chief photographer of the English weekly, *Cine Advance*, and privy to some of Suchitra's private and special moments, once recounted in an interview how she and her husband lived it up in Mumbai during the shooting of *Devdas*.

Life in the Sen household were full of fun and frolic, and parties. Almost every night was a party night, whether the Sen couple were in town or holidaying. Home was filled with warmth with unending celebrations, especially at Diwali, Christmas and Suchitra's famous Lakshmi Puja. Easter cakes were distributed to everyone in school and trucks were hired after Durga Puja and Saraswati Puja to immerse the idols.

Daughter Moon Moon remembers her mother being very glamorous off-screen, too. At times, her mother would be dressed in black lace and red feathers for a night-out.

Life came to an abrupt halt after the untimely death of Dibanath Sen in 1970. The loss brought about a great transformation in Suchitra. Despite her style and sophistication, Suchitra embraced a life of simplicity, even austerity to ward off undue attention. Journalist Amitabha Chaudhuri mentions how he was pleasantly surprised to discover her spartan lifestyle at this time—her room had only a small wooden cot and minimum furniture.

Somewhat imperious and formidable, Suchitra encouraged the public perception that she was 'a cut above the rest'. 'Madam,' as she was called, lived life on her own terms, something quite extraordinary given the social constraints of her time. She is even known to have turned down an offer to work with Satyajit Ray because his conditions did not suit her. Given the success of *Pather Panchali* and Ray's stature, that was indeed a bold decision.

Aparna Sen recalls that when she entered the film industry, Suchitra was already a celebrity. Asit Chowdhury, a producer, had thrown a party at Grand Hotel in Kolkata to honour Suchitra for winning the best-actor award in Moscow International Film Festival for *Saat Pake Bandha.* Suchitra surprised the audience by suddenly ripping actor Soumitra Chatterjee's shirt off his chest, as she had done in the film! In those days, such a stunt could have been carried off only by a personality, such as Suchitra, believes Aparna Sen.

It would be impossible define the woman that Suchitra was those days—sometimes childlike, sometimes the diva, at times the complete homebody, and at other times the blazing cinestar. Her charm in each of these avatars captivated and mesmerised her admirers. She was an enigma.

There was also a bewitching duality about Suchitra's personality. She could be snooty and reprimanding at times, and loving and soft the very next moment. While the woman in her was well aware of her charms, she did not use it to entice others. However, she was certainly impish, a quality that endeared her to others. Author and friend Gopal Krishna Roy, in his book *Romantic Juti* recounts that the times she used her mesmerising smile to ward off inquisitive questions about her personal life. Stories of how she dealt with men who dared to cross the Rubicon also abound. It is believed that she slapped a Mumbai producer who made a pass at her on the sets.

Old timers remember her as a thin girl with beautiful expressive eyes, a lovely smile and long hair, when she started acting. She had a striking face that matured into something more fascinating over a period of time. Dilip Kumar, who worked with her in *Devdas,* was reportedly captivated by the combination of her beauty and brains. His admiration for Suchitra is believed to have irked Vyjayanthimala, who played Chandramukhi in the film.

Suchitra also had the unique ability to convincingly portray both an Indian girl as well as the anglicised city sophisticate. While she was excellent in her heel-trotting, skirt-attired persona of Rina Brown in *Saptapadi,* her role of a devotee, united with the lord in *Bhagaban Shrikrishna Chaitanya,* (1953) spoke equally well of her acting abilities.

Suchitra, the actor and Roma (as she was called by those close to her), albeit one, were distinct from each other. Though Roma lived a private life like any other married woman, cinema was an inseparable part of her existence. She was a caring and soft person, a true friend who fussed around her friends, but was acutely conscious of her alter-ego, the 'Suchitra Sen' persona. A gracious host one minute, she could be completely unapproachable the next minute if provoked.

Suchitra has often been described as temperamental by people who have worked with her. 'Amitabha Chaudhuri, former journalist and close associate of Suchitra Sen, observed that despite being temperamental and moody, Suchitra had some very good friends who she stood by and supported whole-heartedly in their hour of need. Filmmaker and poet Gulzar recalls how she never forgot that he liked a glass of cold milk and always offered him one.

Director Pinaki Mukhopadhay, recounted an incident that happened when he was working with Suchitra in *Alo Amar Alo* (1971). Suchitra asked him to visit her at home to discuss the script. When he reached her house, he realised that she had no intention of discussing the script. Instead, she wanted him to see a doctor! Cholera was rampant those days and Suchitra knew that being a film director, Pinaki Mukhopadhay was a busy man who spent much of his time outdoors.

As soon as Mukhopadhay arrived, she ordered a doctor who she had summoned, to give him a cholera injection. Dumbfounded, Mukhopadhay tried to wriggle out of the situation due to his innate aversion to medicines. But Mrs Sen's persistence paid off and he was inoculated. Such was Suchitra with people she cared for.

Probably the transition from Suchitra the actor to Suchitra the diva was responsible in part for her temperamental behaviour. Sabitri Chatterjee, a renowned Bengali actress of yesteryears, recounts instances when at the height of Suchitra's popularity, several producers and directors would hurry to hold an umbrella to 'Mrs Sen'.

Film critic Ranjan Bandopadhay had famously termed her 'vintage wine'. MF Hussain drew a sketch of her based on her pictures and named it 'Mystique'. Derek Malcolm, one of Britain's best-loved critics who had a special connection with Bengali cinema, observed how Suchitra had this 'still' quality about her. She did not have to do a lot of 'acting.' She 'underplayed' her role and, of course, looked wonderful.

If on the one hand, Suchitra was warm, on the other hand she was also very possessive about the people she liked. One such person was Dhiren Deb. Suchitra would often ask him to accompany her on her outdoor shoots. He recollects that when they went to Mumbai together for the shooting of *Devdas,* he had decided to stay with Mala Sinha, an acquaintance. He soon found out that it did not go down well with Suchitra.

She enjoyed being admired and adored, but retreated into a shell the moment someone tried to peek into her private world. No one was allowed to intrude into her private space. She guarded that fiercely. The media had no access to her inner circle and she enjoyed her reclusive film star status. She maintained a demeanour that conveyed that she would rather be known for her work than for anything else. Kana Basu Mishra, a friend, writer and media person who had visited Suchitra's parents' home in Shantiniketan, wrote how Suchitra's reputation kept her away from her parents as well; she did not meet them till many years after her rise to fame.

Stories abound on how she stopped the filming of *Grihadaha* just because she did not want to shoot in the presence of outsiders (including some technicians on the sets). On repeatedly being coaxed by Uttam, the producer of the film, she resumed work. The same Suchitra was putty in the hands of those she liked, provided of course that she was in the right frame of mind. Dhiren Deb recollects an occasion when he had told her he wanted to click a photograph of hers that would drive the youth crazy. Suchitra calmly walked to her bathroom and called Dhiren Deb in. Clad in a towel, she posed for him. When he asked if a 'No Kiss' could be written on her cheek, she allowed her daughter Moon Moon to do the honour. The photograph truly drove the fans crazy.

Suchitra was reluctant to talk about her personal life even with trusted confidantes. Gopal Krishna Roy remarks in his book that Suchitra would neither corroborate nor dismiss the rumours about her personal life. At times it was hard to make out whether she was serious or joking. Suchitra weighed her words carefully before replying to a query about her professional or personal life, with the diplomacy and dignity worthy of a star of her stature.

When asked to comment on her relationship with Uttam, she is known to have famously said that they were neither brother-sister, nor lovers. She was his *'Priyo Bandhobi'* ('good friend' in Bengali; the eponymous film [1970] they acted in). To whether Uttam had ever tried to influence her to act in more films, she had replied, 'Why should he? He would never question my personal preferences.'

People have often spoken of her 'ego' problems, especially with Uttam during the making of both *Harano Sur* and *Agnipariksha.*

Suchitra was also impulsive and at times childish, in search of the little joys of life. Gopal Krishna Roy relates that once, Suchitra had a sudden urge to visit the Dakshineshwar Temple. Roy was surprised and cautioned her that she may be mobbed in the crowded temple. But Suchitra would not listen. Well covered, somehow they managed to have a *darshan* (visitation) of the deity, but had to make a dash for the car when some admirers pounced on her. In the safety of the car, Suchitra decided she wanted *shingaras* (an Indian snack). While her *shingaras* and tea were being brought, she made small talk with a beggar. And she left only after she'd had her snack.

Suchitra's acting skills were inevitably compared with those of other female leads of her time. She drew flak for being melodramatic sometimes. While such criticism disheartened her, she maintained a studied silence and repeatedly proved her critics wrong with performances that were anything but lacklustre. Sabitri Chatterjee confirmed in an interview that Suchitra used to be perturbed at being considered a pretty face while Sabitri received accolades for her acting prowess. Suchitra, too, wished to be acknowledged more for her performances.

She faced many difficulties in life. Insiders talk of terrible fights with husband Dibanath Sen over his constant drinking and his suspicion of her liaisons with several film personalities, including her friend and producer Asit Sen. The marriage was a turbulent one and she shouldered the responsibility of bringing up daughter Moon Moon single-handedly. Dhiren Deb, who witnessed many such fights, recalls an occasion when Dibanath Sen tried to attack Asit Sen with a knife, a disaster which Suchitra somehow averted.

Like most other actors, she was linked to producers and actors. While these rumours only fuelled marital discord, none of these were ever corroborated. In fact, her much-discussed relationship with Uttam, her co-star of over 30 films, was never acknowledged or even mentioned by Suchitra. She remained dignified, portraying a formal screen image in keeping with her standing in society as a respectable actor.

Quietly warding off criticism and manipulations, Suchitra survived in the film industry by the sheer dint of her character and hard work, largely on her terms. Perhaps, her wariness stemmed from the fact that being friendly and open to people would result in people taking advantage of her. The reserved exterior and aloofness in fact helped keep such people at bay.

The woman in Suchitra was always caring and home-loving. She was very close to her daughter Moon Moon. Though Moon Moon was studying in the UK, the two would visit each other often. During vacations, Moon Moon would also regularly visit her mother on the sets. Despite her busy schedule, Suchitra found time to inspire and encourage her daughter's creative pursuits. The daughter remembers a time when Suchitra was so happy with Moon Moon's artistic talents that she arranged for the best teachers to groom her and encouraged her to have her own shows. Suchitra, however, was completely against Moon Moon joining films and was visibly upset when she chose a career in acting. With her daughter growing up, Suchitra finally cut down on her acting assignments.

One of the few people Suchitra was close to in the film industry was Kanan Devi, a highly talented actress of yesteryears. Over the years, the two artistes had developed a strong bond. Once, following a marital crisis, Suchitra left home with Moon Moon in a fit of anger, and moved to Spencer's, a renowned hotel. At this time of distress, she spoke to Kanan Devi, who took Suchitra to her home, where she stayed for over a month with her daughter and sister Runa. Later, she patched up with her husband and returned home.

Suchitra stoically put up with a very stressful marriage and the strain of keeping her home intact for a long time. But when the news of her husband's death on 29th December, 1970, was broken to her on the sets of *Megh Kalo* (1970), she seemed shattered. Sabitri Chatterjee confirmed that Suchitra used to be rather lively and cheerful in her heydays. A tremendous transformation came over her after Dibanath Sen passed away. And over time, she became a total recluse. Indeed she went to great lengths to remain so. It is believed that when she answered phone calls, she would often speak with a Hindi accent as though she were the maid, and tell the callers to call back later as 'Memsahib' was busy! This was discovered inadvertently by her friend Kana Basu Mishra.

Most people who have worked with her refuse to comment on her, partly out of respect for her wish to remain a recluse. After observing Suchitra repeatedly shying away from house guests, Moon Moon Sen and her daughters realised that Suchitra prefers isolation.

As the screen goddess of yesteryears, now in her 80s, Suchitra retired in 1978 to a cloistered existence in her Ballygunge Circular Road residence in South Kolkata. Till 1998, there were reports of people seeing her visiting her lawyer Barin Dhar's house in the evening, donning her famed sunglasses, with a handkerchief and a small purse in hand. She would cover her head in a scarf and use her daughter Moon Moon's car to do so since her own car would be recognised immediately.

Veteran actress and Uttam Kumar's companion, Supriya Devi, claims to have seen Suchitra in 2002, disguised in a black dress that covered her completely, years after her retirement from public life. 'Suchitra asked me if I had recognised her, and I recognised the voice at once.'

There has been immense curiosity about her untimely retirement and her looks. Incessant reporting by TV channels on her being admitted to the Belle Vue Clinic, Kolkata, twice, in 2007, and more recently in 2012 for a wrist fracture surgery, proves that Suchitra has truly achieved an enigmatic cult status. Ironic as it may seem, in 2007, when Suchitra was admitted to Belle Vue Clinic, she was allotted a bed just two beds away from where Uttam had lain in 1980 before passing away.

Attending doctors Kranti Bhushan Bakshi and Sapan Pal were aware of their immense responsibility towards their celebrity patient and chose to ignore all media queries on what she looked like. Pradip Tandon, CEO of Belle Vue Clinic, who had seen her, volunteered to only say that except for some weight gain she was much like her former self. Suchitra had strict instructions that if her privacy was not ensured, she would leave right away. Non-Bengali nurses attended on her, and all the staff on that particular floor had to deposit their mobile phones before attending to her or even going close to where she was.

Today, she spends most of her time in meditation. She prefers to live in her own private world, away from prying eyes. She seems to have completely sliced off a part of her life and assumed an identity that she had long been searching for. This identity seems to have finally brought her the inner peace that she had always craved for. It is said that she does not like the mention of her film career nor does she watch her films. Her only tie with the world of films is because of her granddaughters Raima and Riya, who are actresses as well. The last time she was seen in public was when she stood in a queue to get her photograph taken for a voter's identity card in Kolkata.

There have been repeated attempts to draw her out of her self-imposed isolation, but the lady refused to indulge even the highest quarters. In 2005, people wondered whether she would come out to accept the Dada Saheb Phalke award, for which she had been considered, provided she accepted it in person. Suchitra declined the honour.

Religion has always played a major role during important phases of Suchitra's life. She became a devotee of Ramakrishna Paramhansa early, and took *deeksha* (initiation in to an order) from Swami Bireshwaranandaji, with whom she developed a very close relationship. She is known to visit the Dakshineshwar Temple and Belur Math often in search of spiritual solace. People in Belur Math have often been surprised at her total surrender to the Almighty and sudden detachment from the world of films at the peak of success.

But to those who really know Suchitra the person, her charitable and pious bent of mind are nothing new. Besides being religious, Suchitra has always contributed as much as she could for causes that she believes in. At a time when she no longer wished to make public appearances, she made an exception by appearing at a function on the condition that ₹ 1000 be paid to Bidhan Chandra Ray's tuberculosis clinic. On 31st December, 1963, a friendly cricket match was organised with filmstars to raise money for soldiers wounded in the 1962 Indo-China war. Suchitra bought a cricket bat during the auction to help the cause. Biswajit, an actor of yesteryears remembers Suchitra as an extremely reserved person. He recalls visiting her while organising a show to help the victims of the North Bengal floods in the 1970s. While Suchitra graciously helped with money, she declined the request for a public appearance.

Interestingly, Uttam and Suchitra both shared a love for a simple life, more so towards the latter half of their lives. If Uttam became philosophical and world weary before his death, Suchitra, too, moved away from her normal routine life and turned to spirituality.

Her compulsive need to maintain her privacy has done little to lessen the invasion into her privacy. Rumour has it that an ageing Suchitra is afflicted with a mysterious disease. There have been speculations about bone-marrow transplant in the 1980s at the Tata Memorial Hospital, Mumbai, following which she is supposed to have suffered from skin-related problems and hair loss. Several other reports suggest that she underwent blood transfusion abroad for treatment of septicaemia.

Be it the wish to remain ever youthful in the eyes of the public, or in eternal mourning for Uttam, the more Suchitra tries to protect her privacy, the more speculations about her abound. While Dr Kamal Hussain, a psychiatrist observes that a wish for total seclusion is not a healthy approach; it indicates a narcissistic personality and an obsessive need to keep the earlier public image intact in the memory of her fans. Dr Debashish Ray, a close associate suggests that her spiritual evolution may have necessitated seclusion.

Moon Moon is reluctant to speak about her mother and says, 'I understand that people want to know about her. But she doesn't like too many queries about her life; let us all respect her decision.'

Surprisingly, and perhaps, intentionally, Suchitra never set foot in Tollygunge Studio after her retirement. Whether this was her way of paying her last respects to her friend Uttam, or a simple decision of keeping away from memories shall forever remain a mystery.

Much like Bollywood screen-goddess Madhuri Dixit, Uttam had an infectious smile that endeared him to the audience almost immediately. When Uttam occupied screen space, little else mattered. The man and his magnetism were such that whatever role he was in, his presence had an overriding impact. Uttam may not have possessed the grandeur of Dilip Kumar or the talent of Soumitra Chatterjee, but people simply adored him.

Uttam's charisma was multi-dimensional. It was a combination of that famous smile with its touch of mischievousness and vulnerability, his aura of indisputable honesty and dependability, his versatility as an actor, his grasp over the technicalities of cinema and above all, his inimitable 'Bengaliness'.

Ajoy Kar, a mentor of Uttam, described him as 'the soul of a film', and aptly so. The sheer range of characters he portrayed, his effortless performances, his image of an incorrigible romantic and his bewitching presence made him hugely popular among the masses, without so much even taking into account his creative calibre and other inputs into filmmaking. Uttam infused something, be it sophistication or a rustic charm or even carefree abandon, into every role he essayed. The contrasting qualities were so well-integrated that his performance was ecstasy for the audience.

Born as Arun Kumar Chatterjee on 3rd September, 1926 in North Kolkata to Satkori Chatterjee and Chapala Devi, he grew up in a joint family. The child was fondly called Uttam by his maternal grandfather, a name not much liked by his mother. However, when the family '*kulguru*' (head priest), Sri Purna Sanyasi saw the three-month-old Uttam smiling at him, he predicted that this name would bring him great fame. Thus started the journey of Uttam—the '*Mahanayak*' (great hero) of Bengali cinema. His foray into films was not pre-planned, though acting was a hobby that he pursued, off and on, from childhood.

His father, the chief operator in Metro cinema, was a disciplinarian who did not want his children to neglect their studies for the love of theatre. His mother, whom Uttam loved dearly, belonged to an affluent family and was more culturally inclined. Uttam had two brothers, Barun and Tarun, and a sister named Putul. The extended family lived in Girish Mukherjee Road.

The whole family was involved in theatre. Suhrid Samaj, the family owned theatre group, gave young Arun a platform to start early. The group that staged several amateur shows within a small community was Arun's first learning ground for anything related to acting. Whenever a production was staged, the entire household bustled with activity. While the men acted, the women served as the audience. A fascinated Uttam missed many study sessions to watch theatre rehearsals. His sister Putul made quite an impression on the young Uttam. Putul was the first person to recognise his love for acting. 'If you learn acting well, you can become a great actor,' she had said. To Uttam's grief, Putul died early and could not see her little brother's rise to fame as she had predicted.

Uttam was interested in most creative activities; he sketched from time to time, made posters for the plays of his theatre group; he even started a club called 'Lunar Club' with his friends. His parents were quite worried that his artistic pursuits would affect his studies but they never exercised extreme discipline to control him, something that reflected in the calm disposition of the actor.

Uttam completed his early education from Chakraberia School, matriculated from the reputed South Suburban School in Kolkata and got admission in

Government Commercial College (now known as Goenka College). He showed his theatrical talent whenever he got an opportunity. Starting from playing the role of Gayasur in school to roles, such as Kalindi and Sirajudulla in theatre while in college, Uttam came to be recognised as a talented actor. Soon he was involved in serious theatrical productions like *Braja Kanai,* where he acted with Phani Ray. The role fetched him critical acclaim.

Uttam's sensitive mind was disturbed by many events during this time: the death of Rabindranath Tagore, Subhash Chandra Bose's role in the freedom movement and later, the Naxalite movement. After passing out of college in 1945, Uttam realised that he needed to work to support his family, so he joined the port commissioner's office in the cash department on a salary of ₹ 275. He would work during the day and reserve his evenings for theatre and watch shows at Rangmahal, Minerva and Star on the cheapest tickets.

In 1948, he got married to Gauri Devi, despite parental opposition on both sides. Even though the two separated later, Gauri Devi had a tremendous influence on his life. It was her constant encouragement that enabled him to pursue acting amidst all uncertainty. Such was his dedication that he learnt singing, some Urdu, English, horse riding and even lawn tennis, in an attempt to improve his acting skills.

Uttam chanted religious texts like *Chandi* and *Gita,* throughout his life, as he believed that these would help his oratory skills. Obsessed with fitness, he exercised regularly and was interested in *lathi-khela* (sparring with wooden sticks), wrestling and swimming. It is believed after he developed a heart problem, he continued with his walks while a jeep followed him for his safety. He was also the swimming champion at the Bhowanipur Swimming Association for three consecutive years.

Uttam's love for his family and his sense of responsibility towards them remained intact till the last days of his life. Having grown up in a huge joint family, Uttam was attached to most of his family members. His brother's wife and their children remember him as a very doting elder for whom family always came first. Tarun Kumar's daughter Monami, who calls Uttam *Jejan*, recalls that if he went to buy a saree for one of the family members, he ended up buying gifts for almost everyone. He not only provided for them, but also took care of all the household responsibilities.

Most fans wonder whether Uttam, the on-screen romantic hero, was as romantic in real life, too. In an interview towards the latter half of his life, he had, in a rather endearing manner, said that he liked to be pampered by near and dear ones. If someone put out his clothes for him or untied his shoelaces after a tiring day, he would be ecstatic.

It is believed that he celebrated his anniversary with Gauri Devi on 1st June, every year, and would spend the entire day with her. He would sing Rabindra Sangeet for her, mostly his favourite, '*Shedin Dujone Dulechhinu Bone*' and gift her sarees and jewellery that he would have handpicked for her. The ever-indulgent romantic that he was, he used to throw lavish parties on such occasions. It was hardly surprising that there was mutual love and respect between him and Gauri Devi even after he left home to live with Supriya Devi.

Uttam was linked to many of his leading ladies and acknowledged his emotional attachment with two women—Sabitri Chatterjee and Suchitra Sen. But it was Supriya Devi with whom he lived till he breathed his last.

Sabitri Chatterjee apparently proclaimed that she did love Uttam, but she could not hope to marry him as he was a married man. Supriya Devi on the other hand said in her autobiography that in spite of living under the same roof for 17 years, their relationship was platonic, based on a shared passion for cinema, mutual love and respect. Much as she would have liked to have a family with him, she, too, had to respect his status in the society. On his part, Uttam adopted Supriya Devi's daughter as his own to give the relationship respect and stability. The authenticity of this adoption was later questioned by Uttam Kumar's wife Gauri Devi.

Uttam's love for his mother Chapala Devi was legendary. He would visit his family home every morning before leaving for work, even after he had shifted to Supriya Devi's Moira Street residence. Uttam loved his son Gautam dearly and did everything he could to support and secure his future. Gautam recalls how his father would pamper him with the best of toys. Uttam was not inclined towards sending his son away for studies. However, given the nature of his job and the filmy atmosphere at home, he thought it was best to keep Gautam away from it all and sent him to a residential school in Darjeeling. Later, he set up a pharmacy business for Gautam.

There were two distinct sides to Uttam. His empathy with suffering and his eagerness to help the needy earned Uttam tremendous respect in the industry from producers, directors, senior and junior artistes, alike. He never forgot his own origins and his struggles in the past and always encouraged young, upcoming actors, even helping those who were out of work. Uttam also empathised with the plight of directors and producers—a quality that made him the first choice for producers and directors.

Perhaps, no other actor has done as much for the industry and its co-workers as Uttam did. Through his Shilpi Sansad, he toiled to provide security for retired actors and actresses. He organised charity functions and got the entire industry involved in this cause.

Democratic by nature, Uttam also took a stand against differential treatment meted out to actors not as famous as him. Stories of how he forced producers to serve good food to all the unit members and protested against serving the unit boys food on leaves, instead of plates, are still recounted in studios. He was truly a godfather to the Bengali film industry with a lifelong commitment to improving the working conditions of the underprivileged.

Uttam was also a very religious man who could be superstitious on occasions. He was keenly interested in occult and could make astrological *kundali*s (horoscopes). It is believed that he shifted back to his Girish Mukherjee Road residence where he grew up, from his newly constructed Alipore house, because the latter seemed inauspicious with a trail of flops attached to it. Like co-star Suchitra, Uttam also performed Lakshmi Puja, (worship of the Goddess of Wealth) in a traditional way, with great pomp. A large-hearted man, the doors of his house remained open for all, on most occasions

His popularity however, imposed certain restrictions on his movements. He could visit a place of his liking—a friend's house or the theatre—only late at night. The star in him, however, believed in maintaining some exclusivity.

The public expected a hero to be extraordinary and Uttam believed in not overexposing himself. It seems he once saw Subhendu Chatterjee, a budding hero at that time, paying his bills at a gas station. When they met next, Uttam reminded the young man to refrain from such activities so as to retain his image. He himself declined offers for advertisements, except once when he lent his name to Kole Biscuit Company.

However, while Uttam maintained his star persona off-screen, he challenged the same on-screen. There he was, the lovable hero, always suave and polished, yet someone very close to a common man's heart.

A talented and creative soul, Uttam was always attracted to various aspects of culture. Music and song were an important part of his life. He had taken classical music lessons from Nidan Bandopadhyay and sang Rabindra Sangeet beautifully. He had also recorded some songs; a song by Uttam goes, '*Ei Mon Jochonai Ongo Bhijiye, Esho Na Golpo Kori*'. Early in his career, he gave music lessons to supplement his income, and it was through music that he met his wife Gauri Devi. Uttam would play the harmonium and practise the songs that were to be filmed on him. Perhaps, it is this perfectionist in him that made the songs picturised on him seem so natural.

In an interview, Manna Dey had said, 'Uttam's expressions for each of my songs were so brilliant that I often wonder whether they are my songs or his.' He had added, 'As he could sing very well himself, he knew the exact movements that would match the rhythm of the song.' Manna Dey recalls seeing Uttam during his morning walk with a tape recorder, listening to the songs of *Antony Phiringi* (1967), trying to master them. Such dedication was indeed rare.

Uttam tried his hand at music direction, too, and successfully directed music for two films—*Sabyasachi* (1948) and *Kaal Tumi Aleya* (1966). His voice has always been considered one of his strengths. Women swooneed over his melodious baritone and he lent his voice to the narration of many films. At the peak of his popularity, Uttam was requested by Akash Bani, Kolkata, to deliver the *Chandi Path* for *Mahalaya* (an invocation to Goddess Durga to visit her earthly abode), a tradition that had always been conducted by Birendra Krishna Bhadra. The programme, however, was severely criticised later and Uttam is said to have apologised to Birendra Krishna Bhadra in person, for his failure to keep up the tradition as efficiently.

Though Uttam's love for music was well-known, few know that the versatile superstar was also interested in literature. Be it as a producer or as an actor, he made it a point to understand the nuances and details about the characters of the story. Often he would visit the scriptwriter's house to discuss with him details about the character. Uttam was also known to carry along works of Rabindranath Tagore, Bishnu De and others, to read in his free time. The actor used to have literary discussions with Hemanta Kumar and his producers and directors whenever the situation permitted. He found time to attend *sahitya sabha*s (literary meets) along with poet Dinesh Gangopadhyay and actor Pahari Sanyal.

As an extension of his passion for literature, Uttam was actively involved in the scripts of his films. Few know that Uttam had also written scripts for Subodh Ghosh's *Sashanchampa* and Tarun Roy's *Nuner Putul Sagare*—both short stories.

Throughout his life, Uttam loved people and they loved him tremendously in return. Often referred to as '*Guru*' by the masses, he belonged to a rare group of men who gave back to society far more than what he had received. He did not remain in the cocoon of stardom. An intelligent actor, he knew exactly what the audience wanted and delivered just that. Astonishingly, Uttam was one actor who brought in international standards of acting within the framework of Bengali cinema

Though initially named 'flop master' because of a string of early flops, Uttam's circumstances improved dramatically, and he became immensely popular for his roles as a romantic hero, especially with Suchitra.

His experimentation with other roles did not go unnoticed either, and with age he mellowed into a successful character-actor. Acting in Satyajit Ray classics, such as *Nayak* (1966) and *Chiriyakhana* was a turning point in his career. So were other films including *Basu Parivar*, *Stree* (1972), *Antony Firingi* and *Amanush* (1975). He was influenced by Chhobi Biswas as an actor and considered PC Barua as his idol.

Averse to the mannerisms of stage-acting of the time, Uttam was among the few actors to introduce a natural style of acting, with his performances getting due recognition and acclaim from the best of film critics, in time. In a solemn observation, Satyajit Ray noticed that even in films where the director's calibre was questionable, Uttam tried his best to contribute to the overall success of the film; with the better ones he simple excelled.

Born lucky, Uttam had the kind of death he wished for. He was just 54 when he died of a massive heart attack during the shooting of *Ogo Bodhu Shundori* (1981) on 24th

July, 1980. It is said that he had run up huge debts during the production of *Chhoti Si Mulaqat* (1967), his Waterloo. Though he managed to pay off the debts, the experience took a toll on his health. Also, apparently, the news of being dropped from Tapan Sinha's *Banchharaamer Bagan* (1980) left him dejected.

Interviews given during this time indicate a lonely man, restless and frustrated, trying to cope with the excruciating demands of a success-driven industry. The near-absence of people who genuinely cared for him left a void within him. Around this time, when his son Gautam expressed his wish to be a film actor, the doting father is said to have called him to the window and pointed to a sleeping rickshaw-puller, saying, 'Even he sleeps better, and is more at peace with himself than me.' Discouraged by his father, Gautam abandoned the idea of acting.

The milling crowds at his funeral were a testimony to the popularity of this great artiste. His death was mourned by thousands of Bengalis across the world. Till date, Bengali cinema has not recovered from the loss of Uttam, nor has it produced an actor and a wholesome entertainer like him. In the words of Satyajit Ray, 'It is the demise of a leading light of the Bengali film industry... There isn't, and there won't be another hero like him.'

The passage of time has not dimmed his memories, and tributes continue to pour in. A metro railway station in Kolkata was named after him and recently postage stamps honouring him were also released. Uttam awards have been established to honour film personalities. An Uttam Mancha, located in South Kolkata, stages plays and screens his films regularly. *'Oti Uttam'* (a cut above the rest) was a weekly programme named after him.

South Kolkata honoured the actor with a life-size statue near the Tollygunge Metro Station, close to the studios where he worked.

Till date, his make-up room at New Theatres Studio is maintained as though he could walk in any time. It is a simple room with a wall mirror, a dressing table, a small divan, a chair, a shelf for clothes and a pair of wooden sandals that the actor used. A portrait of Uttam sits on the table and incense sticks burn in memory of the *Mahanayak*.

4

Lights, Camera, Action

When the creation was new and all the stars shone in their first splendour,
The gods held their assembly in the sky and sang,
'Oh, the picture of perfection! The joy unalloyed.'
But one cried of a sudden,
'It seems that somewhere there is a break in the chain of light
And one of the stars has been lost.'

Rabindranath Tagore

Did Uttam and Suchitra fight amongst themselves, throw tantrums at each other, or were they the best of friends, soul mates or more intense and intimate than that? Were they thorough professionals or did they allow their personal lives to intrude into their professional space, once in a while? And more importantly, was their off-stage persona as charismatic as their on-screen presence?

Any director, producer or a film journalist, of the 1960s, would vouch for Uttam's and Suchitra's devotion to their craft. Suchitra is believed to have expressed the desire to complete her work even the day her husband died. Comparable incidents abound, as well, about Uttam's dedication to work.

Among the many passions the duo shared, the love of films and the wish to do something different each time seemed to be a common denominator. In their distinct ways, both stars brought not only a great degree of charm but also professionalism to their roles. It is difficult to not notice the spontaneity and the consummate ease with which they acted their part; how much they added to each other's presence. Their unique professional chemistry ultimately became a hallmark of their greatness as actors. Perhaps, this professional integrity and dynamism made Suchitra and Uttam what they were. Instead of standing out as two formidable rivals, they blended their individualities beautifully, to become the most celebrated off-screen pair, ever.

Suchitra used to be addressed as 'Sir' by Gulzar, not as much out of respect as out of humour. While working on *Aandhi* (1975) Gulzar resorted to calling her 'Sir', in retaliation to her persistently calling him so, despite being friends. Such was Suchitra's persona.

Suchitra made her debut with *Sesh Kothay* (1952). Since this film was never released, her first release was *Saat Number Kayedi* (1953).

Circumstances that led to her decision to enter films are unclear. It is believed that Suchitra convinced her conservative father-in-law Adinath Sen about her acting potential and her desire to make it big in films. However, when she was offered *Sanket* (1951) by Ardhendu Mukherjee, she turned it down, citing domestic problems. Chances are that her daughter, Moon Moon, was very young at that time, and needed looking after.

Suchitra went on to become the first Bengali actor to be designated '*Mahanayika*', (great actress). Earlier, most actresses were categorised as '*nayika*' (actress—associated with good or serious acting) and '*taraka*' (star performer). Suchitra was a mix of both and therefore commanded a more exalted status. That Suchitra became a name to reckon with, however, cannot obliterate the fact that her initial entry into films was tentative for the kind of films and the roles she was offered. *Srabana Sandhya* (1974) was released 22 years after Suchitra had established her star status. Suchitra herself was rather sceptical about the audience's reaction to this early film by her but to her great relief, it did not run for long.

For someone who began a career with insignificant roles, Suchitra achieved stupendous success in Bengali cinema, with an extraordinary career graph. In 1963, she was honoured with the first International Best Actress award for an Indian woman in the Moscow International Film Festival. The award was given to her for her sensitive portrayal in *Saat Pake Bandha.* In 1958, Suchitra was invited to London by the BBC for a talk on Bengali cinema and her role in it.

For two decades, starting from 1953, Suchitra paired with Uttam to give the Bengali film industry its first ever hit pair. The first film they starred in together was the riotously hilarious, *Sare Chuattor.*

Director Asit Sen, a confidante, feels that neither Suchitra nor her critics imagined she would become a legend one day. A girl who spoke with an East Bengali accent, Suchitra began her career with some small roles in frothy comedies like *Atom Bomb* (1954) and *Kajori* (1953). Director Sukumar Dasgupta, however, confirms that it was Suchitra's dedication and total involvement in her character that enabled her to not only get into the characters, but also to totally neutralise her accent in a matter of days.

Suchitra's success can be attributed to her sense of style, glamour and carriage, grit and determination to prove herself, alloyed with author-backed roles. Her face was perfect for black-and-white soft focus shots. When she romped around as the happy-go-lucky girl in *Saptapadi*, it made our hearts skip a beat. When, as a bride, she lip sync-ed '*Tumi Je Amar...*', in *Harano Sur*, the world seemed to stand still.

It must be said, however, that both Uttam and Suchitra owed much of their popularity to each other! Interestingly, they both maintained their public behaviour distinct from their private lives though it was their on-screen chemistry that left the audience asking for more.

Suchitra was Bengal's first glamour queen. As Khagen Roy, director of *Amar Bou* notes, 'The Bengali audience learnt the meaning of glamour from her.' The fact that she was as glamorous on-screen as she was off-screen added to her aura. While other popular heroines before and during her time, like Kanan Devi (singing star) and Sadhana Basu (dancer-cum-actor) were also very attractive, Suchitra lent a new dimension to glamour—she was reserved and controlled. He adds, 'Suchitra was the epitome of glamour. For someone like Suchitra, just dressing up was not essential to maintaining or portraying her glamour.' Once she became the darling of millions, her every move, twitch of the lip, hairstyle and the nylon sarees she wore on-screen, became a rage.

A pathbreaker in many ways, in her first colour film *Pothe Holo Deri* (1957), she wore several colourful nylon sarees which set a trend among fashionistas. Few know that Suchitra had once modelled for Bata Shoes. The shot for the company's calendar was taken by Wajid Ali, a famous photographer of those times. In an age when modelling was frowned upon, Suchitra was one of the few ladies from a respectable family to model.

Soumitra Chatterjee, her co-star in three films, *Saat Pake Bandha*, *Datta* (1976), and *Pranoy Pasha* (1978) once said of Suchitra, 'I used to observe her on the sets and wonder why there isn't any other like her. In her, one finds a rare combination of beauty and personality.' He further added that Suchitra was intelligent enough to understand camera angles and poses that would make her look good, an awareness that is an asset for any actor. On his experiences of working with her during *Saat Pake Bandha*, Soumitra said he had to visit Mrs Sen's house from time to time, during the shooting, and that they had many interesting conversations. He remembered Suchitra's advice to him to never overexpose himself as an actor, or to do things that would make him accessible to the common man. She had said, 'The viewers should develop interest and curiosity about you.'

Most of Suchitra's directors attribute her success to her dedication and hard work. A thorough professional, she never let her personal problems come in the way of her work. She was also known for punctuality, and always reported on the sets on time. In case she had to cancel a shoot, she would personally inform the director. Though known to be temperamental and moody, she took care to ensure that her directors or producers were not left in the lurch because of her: she refused to sign an exclusive contract with Satyajit Ray because her other producers would have suffered losses. However, some reports suggest that she did not work with Ray because the two stalwarts of Bengali cinema did not share an amicable rapport.

Director Pinaki Mukhopadhay echoes the sentiments of other directors about Suchitra's professionalism and dedication. He talked of an incident during the outdoor shooting of the film *Alo Amar Alo,* in Gopalpur, West Bengal. A sunrise shot was scheduled for one morning. As the sun rises at 6:30 a.m. in Gopalpur, the entire crew had been asked to report earlier. Around 2:30 a.m., Mukhopadhay and his team were woken up by a torch light shining on their sleepy faces: Suchitra was searching for her make-up man so that she could be ready for the shot on time!

On another occasion, when a difference of opinion cropped up between her and Director Pinaki Mukhopadhay during a shoot, she took him aside and asked him not to carry forward their argument beyond the sets so that it would not affect their personal relationship.

When she cared for someone, she rose beyond the stern-madam image to accommodated them in every way possible. Hrishikesh Mukherjee once said that Suchitra, at the peak of her career, worked nearly free to help him start his first film *Musafir.*

Hailing from East Bengal, Suchitra had a pronounced inflection in sharp contrast to the crisp Bengali spoken in West Bengal. She made a determined effort and rectified her accent in a matter of days to fit into the industry she had entered. As an actress totally involved with the character she played, she became aloof and silent as soon as she was on the floor for shooting. This she believed help her immerse herself in the character. At the same time, it made her unapproachable. Those who worked with Suchitra, the perfectionist, remember her asking for every detail of the story, and character of every role she was to play. If she did not like a particular character or a story, she refused it politely.

Says Gopal Krishna Roy, 'Roma had two totally different personalities: she was Roma at home and Suchitra at work. As Roma, she is a doting mother and grandmother. As Suchitra, she is the fascinating filmstar well aware of her charm and personality. In my book, whenever I talk about her personal side, I have addressed her as Roma, and while talking of her professional achievements I have addressed her as Suchitra.'

Though Suchitra was always interested in dance and music, she was supposed to have two left feet. But she was actively involved in the songs and dances picturised on her. Basanta Chowdhury, her co-star in *Megh Kalo,* recalls her involvement in the picturisation of the song *'Ami Aapon Koriya Chaini Tao Tumi To Aapon Hoyechho',* sung by Asha Bhonsle. The song being her personal favourite, she is said to have put in additional effort to do justice to its beauty, lest it be a waste of the singer's talent. As a result, she would often sit with the director and other crew members to arrive at the best way to portray that particular song.

In an eventful career, Suchitra also found time to actually sing, perhaps, as an extension of her chosen career path. Before she became an actress, Suchitra had recorded songs in her voice. Kamal Ghosh of Megaphone relates the interesting twist of events that led to Suchitra recording songs for his company. In 1958, his company was going though a crisis. It had not come up with new records in the previous seven years, and he decided to bring out something different. When he approached Suchitra for recording songs for his company, she immediately agreed. Ghosh was very impressed by Suchitra's dedication and the hard work she had put into the recording. She recorded two songs: *'Amar Notun Ganer*

Nimantrane Ashbe Ki/Amay Tumi Ager Moton Bhalo Bashbe Ki' and *'Bone Noy Aaj Mone Hoy Jeno/Ronger Agun Praney Legeche'*. The songs were well-received, though Ghosh acknowledges that Suchitra would have done better had the songs been simpler and not as classical.

Director Sukumar Dasgupta recalls his first impression of Suchitra as 'an amazingly beautiful woman with the attitude of a war veteran.' He thinks that her killer instinct, the wish to constantly improvise and improve herself, and her determination that became the driving force behind her success. She worked in 60 films, 53 in Bengali, and seven in Hindi. Her phenomenally successful films include *Harano Sur, Saptapadi, Saat Pake Bandha, Sapmochan* (1955), *Devdas, Deep Jweley Jai, Agnipariksha* and *Aandhi.*

Suchitra was hailed by critics for the first time for her touching performance as Bishnupriya in *Bhagaban Sri Krishna Chaitanya* (1954). Directed by Debaki Bose, Suchitra herself has acknowledged that she would not have been the first choice for the film, but for the insistence of Bose. Bose was instrumental in bringing out a Suchitra that no one had imagined. The film established her as an actress of calibre.

Incidentally, Suchitra's portrayal of Bishnupriya turned out to be even more powerful and sensitive than Bose had imagined. The film holds a special place in Suchitra's heart because for the first time, her spiritual nature was recognised, a dimension which came to the fore much later in her life. Suchitra is believed to have once said, 'Ever since I played the role of Bishnupriya, I have become fearless; it is as if someone is governing my actions.'

Box-office records speak volumes on the Suchitra-Uttam cinematic pairing. Though their biggest hits include

Sagarika, Saptapadi, Harano Sur, Har Mana Har, Indrani and *Bipasha* (1962), it was *Agnipariksha* by the Agradoot Group that really got the couple going. *Agnipariksha* saw Suchitra come of age in her performance. Then on, she gave only fine and mature performances.

After a string of successful films, the Uttam and Suchitra brand become a money-spinner in Bengal. This frustrated both stars because they wished to prove their mettle individually too, and with other co-stars. Added to that were rumours about an affair between the two. Suchitra cut down her assignments with Uttam. Between 1963 and 1968, she did just one film with him—*Grihadaha*—perhaps, in an attempt to prove to her audience and her critics that she had an identity of her own.

About this phase in her career, Gopal Krishna Roy says, 'There might have been professional reasons, but it is a fact that they did have some ego problems from time to time; however, they shared a relationship full of respect for each other, too. Suchitra has often talked about what a large-hearted person Uttam was.'

Most of her films during this period were woman-centric, opposite leading men like Basanta Chowdhury, Bikash Roy and Soumitra Chatterjee. By this time, Suchitra was already an acknowledged actress. The films' commercial prospects largely depended on her. Films like *Hospital* (1960) with Ashok Kumar, *Saat Pake Bandha* with Soumitra Chatterjee and *Deep Jweley Jai* with Basanta Chowdhury were tremendous hits, with fine performances by Suchitra.

Saat Pake Bandha deserves special mention because of Suchitra's sensitive and balanced performance in the role of Archana. The heroine graduates from a young college girl to a married woman and faces a life rife with complications due her mother's interference. Directed by Ajoy Kar, *Saat Pake Bandha* is regarded as a milestone, not only in Suchitra's career, but also in the history of Bengali cinema. The film fetched her international acclaim and the Best Actress Award at the Moscow International Film Festival. Film critics in Moscow said, 'A film of great psychological depth marked by deep analysis of the characters, love of man and professional culture.'

Suchitra acted in seven Hindi films, of which *Aandhi* (1972) and *Mamta* (1966) were successful at the box office. She received critical acclaim for her role as Parvati in Bimal Roy's *Devdas* with Dilip Kumar, and was nominated for the Best Actress award by Filmfare in 1957. Her recognition in Bollywood gave her an edge over other contemporary actors in Bengal, increasing her glamour quotient manifold. Suchitra, however, failed to make a sustained impact in Hindi films. Apart from the language barrier, Suchitra was, perhaps, not accustomed to the ways of Hindi cinema and the expectation of actors there. Hindi cinema also involved different and bolder ways of dressing and a go-getter attitude that she was not comfortable with. Intelligently, she detached herself from Hindi cinema, preferring to remain in Bengali cinema where she was a name to reckon with.

Among the many directors Suchitra worked with, Asit Sen and Ajoy Kar are names associated with her many hits. In Ajoy Kar's *Saat Pake Bandha,* she proved to her critics that she could deliver a hit even on her own steam. *Saptapadi,* another great hit, where she played Rina Brown, fetched her rave reviews.

Asit Sen brought out the best in Suchitra. His films with strong women characters brought out the inner turmoil of his female leads. The director says, 'While working with Roma in *Jiban Trishna* and *Deep Jweley Jai,* I discovered in her a brilliant streak of subtlety for bringing out inner pathos and mental chaos. It was this subtlety that helped bring out a sharply etched character, when rightly employed.' The director thinks Suchitra outperformed, not only his but also her own expectations, in these films. He calls her capacity to transcend given boundaries, unique and rare, and adds, 'She is an all-time great, a class by herself.'

Despite Suchitra's overpowering personality, she excelled in roles that required her to assume softer shades as well, that were neither powerful nor glamorous. In fact, one might consider Suchitra's choice of unusual roles another reason for her extraordinary success. Director Pinaki Mukhopadhay once said, 'Suchitra is very meticulous about her choice of roles, who she works with, including her co-actors and her director. Unless she is fully satisfied, she refuses to work in a film.'

Suchitra's choice of roles indicates a woman with a mind of her own at a time when most actresses were happy doing what they were offered. Most of her roles also highlighted the life of working women, a rare theme those days. She was an army nurse in *Saptapadi*, a doctor in *Harano Sur*, an artiste in *Jiban Trishna*, a nurse again in *Deep Jweley Jai* and a politician in *Aandhi*. She took on the roles of professional women when women's liberation was still an idea imported from the West. Many film historians attribute her choice of strong and diverse roles to the image she had created of herself

She always sought to rise above the tag of a 'pretty face'. She never shied away from taking on challenging characters or experimenting with new multidimensional roles. Her astonishing portrayal of Radha, a hospital nurse in *Deep Jweley Jai*, made the audience cry. Her dual role as the courtesan Pannabai and her daughter Suparna, in *Uttar Falguni* (1963) is indeed memorable for her sensitive portrayal of the characters.

During her long and successful career, Suchitra played numerous author-backed roles, too. Be it Dr Roma Banerjee in *Harano Sur* or Rina Brown in *Saptapadi,* Suchitra took every role and made it her own. Gulzar, who directed *Aandhi,* said few actresses could have lent the dignity Suchitra did to the character of Aarti, the politician in the film.

With her tremendous command over the medium and her personality, Suchitra single-handedly changed the way actors were perceived. At a time when acting in cinema was considered the destiny of women with financial compulsions, Suchitra was an exception. She entered the world of films despite being married to one of the wealthiest and most prestigious families of Kolkata.

Today, many actors comment on the diverse roles that Suchitra played; many have expressed a wish to portray such strong characters. In a poll conducted among new Bengali actors, many had voted for Rina Brown played by Suchitra as their ideal role. Interestingly, Suchitra herself desired to play a particular role, too, of *Chaturanga* created by Rabindranath Tagore. She had said she would be delighted to work with any director who could do justice to a film based on such a role.

Suchitra's lack of inhibitions in romantic scenes, her willingness to embrace and be physically intimate with heroes on the sets was pathbreaking in her times. In *Sagarika,* Suchitra embraced Uttam, who recovered his sight after a prolonged struggle. Such a scene was rather bold by Bengali standards of those days, but Suchitra's acting was highly realistic. Sandip Ray, director and son of Satyajit Ray, had said of her, 'Such screen presence is rare these days.'

Director Asit Sen once remarked, 'It would be stupid to assess a genius like Suchitra with words or a liturgical epithet. She is an actress who seldom needs direction from her directors on how she should act or engineer movement while in film frames. Her intellect is so charming, she can be moulded delicately to personify any character. I cannot say how powerful she is as an actor, but I can definitely affirm that she is a rare quality performer, creating a tremendous depth in her acting.'

Suchitra had her share of brickbats, too. While most actors and directors respect her acting prowess, Pradeep Kumar, her co-star in *Grihadaha,* found her 'self-occupied and selfish as an actor'. Ashok Kumar, who was her friend, said, 'Roma is a good actress, but nothing great. She was inclined towards overdoing it while acting.' In spite of not having worked with Suchitra, Satyajit Ray said of her, 'As an actress, Suchitra is a big name. With regard to acting, she has used her beauty in a nice way.'

A diva and star in her heyday, Suchitra is said to have commanded a price of around ₹ 1 lakh per film. At times she was paid even more than the film's hero. Her tremendous success, coupled with her temperament made her the object of awe. Suchitra tasted commercial success like very few of her contemporaries did. In an age and era where men ruled the roost, Suchitra was the first woman to ride the crest of success and command a brand value that contributed enormously to the marketing of her films.

Much to the chagrin of most heroes except Uttam, Suchitra was all-encompassing and predominant in the films she worked in. Posters of her films carried bigger images of her than those of the heroes. Box-office gurus hailed the films as Suchitra-films most of the time. Only with Uttam did she find an equal in stature and popularity. Most of their films bore the titles of either Uttam-Suchitra or Suchitra-Uttam starrers. If industry gossip is to be believed, Suchitra always desired preferential treatment, whether it was a matter of important scenes, dialogues or featuring her name ahead of Uttam's in the credits of the film. Occasional clashes between the two may have been inevetable.

Industry gossip has it that, at times, Suchitra demanded unheard of amounts as fees from producers who approached her to act in their films. It is believed that in 1962, she charged ₹ 1 lakh to act in *Bipasha* while Uttam was paid ₹ 80,000. After *Bipasha*'s success, Suchitra hiked her fee to ₹ 1.5 lakh per film, much to the consternation of many producers and directors.

When asked about increasing her fees, Suchitra replied that she was tired of everything (probably alluding to her family problems at this point of time) and hence needed to cut down on work. Having said that, she was a woman who often got what she wanted. People were so in awe of her that they were almost afraid of her. Access to her Ballygunge Circular Road residence was limited only to a few filmmakers she approved of! She was known to make her star presence felt. Contemporary actors have said that she had producers bowing to her whims and demands and treating her like royalty.

Suman Gupta, senior journalist and author of *Jejon Achen Nirjane*, writes, 'Like most great actors, she was finicky about her work and would not enact a scene unless she was completely satisfied. Like most artists, she was also temperamental, but probably more than most others.'

Sabitri Chatterjee recounts that during the shooting of *Grihadaha,* she suddenly heard a commotion outside. On enquiring what it was about, she was told that photographer Ajay Biswas had shot a photograph of Suchitra without her permission and this had angered her no end. Suchitra not only removed the film from the camera, but also cancelled the day's shooting!

Her temperament made most filmmakers cautious about approaching her. Her star status ruffled many feathers. One such incident was her much-publicised spat with an editor of the popular film magazine, *Rupmancha.* Suchitra had infuriated the editor by not obliging for a shoot at their office-cum-studio, reinforcing the popular impression that she was a 'moody and stern personality' to deal with, especially where the media was concerned.

While praising her talent, director Hari Das Babu also recalls her temper tantrums on the sets. In fact, he was so frustrated handling the Uttam and Suchitra pair in *Rajlakshmi O Srikanto* that he vowed not to work with them again.

Hari Das Babu said Suchitra would often ask for changes in the dialogue, even on the sets, after shooting had started. Once, on the sets of *Sandhya Deeper Shikha* (1964), when Suchitra wanted similar changes in the dialogue, an irritated Hari Das Babu asked upfront, 'Why is she always creating trouble?' An irate Suchitra marched off to her make-up room in a huff. Fed up with her tantrums, Hari Das Babu had a talk with his producer, saying it would be impossible for him to shoot with her under such circumstances. Suchitra overheard this statement and stopped shooting immediately. Later on, after much persuasion, she resumed shooting and Hari Das Babu was asked by the star-struck producer to apologise to 'Mrs Sen'. Hari Das babu refused, but surprisingly, she did resume work. Without talking to him, she irritated him no end by giving numerous takes, one after another even though the director had not requested for it. Her mission accomplished, she went upto him and touched his feet with an impish smile!

At times Suchitra's aura and popularity landed her in funny situations, too. According to Gopal Krishna Roy, once, when Suchitra was unwell, she called for a doctor of repute to her home. The doctor arrived, sporting fashionable clothes and a heady imported perfume. He examined Mrs Sen thoroughly, and found nothing drastically wrong with her. The doctor's attempts at impressing Mrs Sen left the lady amused!

Whatever be the moods of Suchitra, the diva, her beauty, her immense screen presence and her dedication towards her work remain exemplary. She had a camera-friendly face, but the technicians and cameramen played an important role in highlighting her beauty. Veteran cameraperson Dilip Mukhopadhay had said, 'There was no doubt about the fact that she was beautiful, but apart from that she was very glamorous, too, something rarely found in actresses of her times.' He revealed that she looked best in a three-quarter face frame, something the cameramen who worked with her knew, and they shot her accordingly.

Commanding good treatment from her co-workers, directors and producers, Suchitra ushered in changes in the world of Bengali cinema. Kanan Devi, a senior singer-actor and friend, said, 'Suchitra helped improve the lot of actresses of our times. In one word, she symbolised the revolution of an entire age through her stance.' Her intelligence, steely determination helped her achieve respect and success that very few had imagined possible for a woman. In his memoirs, Tarun Kumar (Uttam's brother) talks about Suchitra's business sense, 'It was she who suggested the idea of hiking their remuneration after a series of hits she and Uttam had delivered.'

Suchitra the professional was a combination of a woman with values and dignity so ingrained in her that she never let others take advantage of her. She respected her co-actors despite being the supreme screen goddess. Whether big or small, she advised everyone to respect their work and maintain their dignity. In spite of her frequent tantrums, she generally did not make her producers or directors suffer, monetarily or otherwise because of her fancies.

Veteran actor Biswajit remembers how Suchitra made him comfortable on the sets of Sushil Majumdar's *Hospital*. When he accidentally broke Suchitra's bangles during the shooting, and was aghast at what he had done, Suchitra reassured him that all was well.

Actor Sumitra Mukherjee said that during the shooting of *Datta*, Suchitra's petticoat was revealed. A young and gullible Sumitra at once bent down to hide it. But Suchitra stopped her, saying, 'That's the job of the assistant who looks after the clothes. While on the sets, you are an actress like me and you should maintain your dignity accordingly.'

Commenting about her intellect and understanding of cinema, noted film critic and author Pradeep Biswas recalls her reactions to a film being screened at the International Film Festival of India (IFFI), in 1982, at Rabindra Sadan, Kolkata. 'While watching *Ceddo* (The Outsider) directed by Ousmane Sembene, her comments, had me dumbstruck and prompted me to notice the critical elements of the movie. She proved the point that great artistes of the world think alike and she was no exception.'

In an attempt to capture Suchitra's life and fascinating foray into cinema, Doordarshan made a documentary on her titled 'Nayika Sangbad' in which several luminaries spoke of her. Several filmmakers, including Aparna Sen, have also tried to document her life and work. The director-actress says that she would have loved to make a feature film on Suchitra. Throughout her career, Suchitra has fought allegations about being a glamorous foil to Uttam. She has been criticised for restricting herself to melodrama. Yet she sought to provide answers to her detractors only through her performances. Perhaps, it was her ultimate answer to her film critics and audience alike when she retired in 1978, after *Pranoy Pasha* flopped. She would no longer be able to play the role of Kironmoyee in *Charitrahin;* the role of *Ma Saradamoi* in biopic on her; a role in a Jatra (Bengali version of folk theatre) even if it were for a single day. She had withdrawn from that world forever.

When Suchitra retired suddenly, many were shocked. She gave none the liberty of questioning her decision and withdrew into quiet seclusion from which she has never emerged. Her fans were highly disappointed at her decision to withdraw from public life. Whether a well-thought out strategy or a simple wish for privacy, Suchitra lives as beautiful and young in the minds of millions of her fans, defying both age and memory. Aparna Sen says,

'Maintaining her image as a youthful icon in the minds of viewers has been Suchitra's biggest triumph!'

When Suchitra lights up the screen in scenes from *Aandhi* or *Devdas,* the pain in her voice is reflected in her eyes, the tender smile that lights up her face in scenes from *Harano Sur* speak of Roma of Pabna who has come a long way both in Bengali and national cinema. In the words of veteran director Tarun Majumdar, 'If Uttam is considered *Mahanayak,* Suchitra is *Mahanayika.* No one can match her presence or popularity in Bengali cinema. She is simply irreplaceable.'

Besides his good looks and winsome smile, Uttam Kumar was a fine combination: actor, producer, director and music director. With an unquenchable thirst for learning and mastery over the medium he worked in, he stood apart from his counterparts who wanted to make it big in show business.

Like most actors of that age, theatre had a great influence on Uttam. Be it watching rehearsals at home for plays staged by his family-owned group, Suhrid Samaj, or enacting Gayasura in school or staging Tagore's *Mukut* as an endeavour of his own home-grown literary group, 'The Lunar Club', Uttam was actively involved with theatre, despite his parents' initial objection. One thing led to another and gradually, even his father had to accept the fact that his son was destined for things other than academics. The young Uttam lost no time in exploring his acting skills and dedicated himself to theatre circles around his home and the city. His role in *Shyamali* (1955) at Star Theatre fetched him acclaim and made him a name to reckon within both theatre and film circles.

Uttam's wish to learn by observation and his quest for perfection, as was the case with Suchitra, helped him become a thorough professional. He was fascinated by the work of all-time great theatre actors, such as Shishir Kumar Bhaduri, Ahindra Chowdhury, Naresh Chandra Mitra and Nirmalendu Lahiri. He would watch them perform whenever possible.

Uttam's dedication to his work, his awareness of his shortcomings and his eagerness to learn has been admired by his seniors and contemporaries alike. When director-cinematographer Bibhuti Laha was asked why he thought so highly of Uttam, he replied, 'I have had the chance to notice him rehearsing the lines of his script even when he was a young boy. I had no doubt in my mind that with his dedication and some guidance, he would outdo others.' Bibhuti Laha had given Uttam two off-beat roles in *Khokababur Prottaborton* (1960) written by Rabindranath Tagore and *Kuhok* (1960) written by Samaresh Basu.

Having made a name for himself in theatre, Uttam started getting offers from films. Now he had to decide whether he would be a theatre or film actor. Uttam chose the latter.

Ironically, Uttam, one of the greatest heroes of Bengali cinema, began his film career as a low-profile extra in films. He secured a small role with the help of his friend Ganesh Mukherjee in a Hindi film, *Mayador.* The *Mahanayak* was paid a princely sum of ₹ 5 for his cameo in the film. While Uttam had pinned his hopes on this film, it was never released. Soon after, he was offered a role in *Drishtidan* (1948) by Nitin Bose. The film was well appreciated and Uttam's talent noticed. However, success continued to elude him despite his hard work. A series of flops including *Kamona* (1949), *Marjada* (1950) and *Sahajatri* (1951) earned him the sobriquet of 'flop master general.'

How the term '*Mahanyak*' came to be associated with him is interesting. In the early stages of his career, once when he took particularly long to give a shot, lingering on to get it perfect, the crew in the studio said jeeringly, 'There's the *Mahanayak* giving his shot!' Little did they know that they were actually addressing the future *Mahanayak* of Bengali cinema.

Uttam had often talked about his days of struggle and painful memories; contracts were snatched away while he was on the verge of signing them or he was replaced by bigger names without notice. After the signing of *Bou Thakuranir Haat* (1953), he was ready to give the mahurat shot when he saw a bigger and more popular actor doing the honours! Uttam didn't forget the embarassment and the humiliation of those early days. Later, when he became a big name, he acknowledged that time and again, some filmmakers had taken advantage of his good nature.

Transcending these initial hiccups, he reached a point when it seemed there was nothing he could not do. And he always acknowledged his indebtedness to two people: his idol Chhobi Biswas, whom he admitted copying in many ways and Santosh Sinha, from whom he learnt to act.

Be it as the aristocratic businessman immersed in his own power in *Nabarag* (1971), or as the poor and diffident Dhiman in *Shilpi* or the inquisitive Bomkesh Bakshi in *Chiriyakhana*, Uttam essayed each role with great care and diversity. It was, however, in *Basu Parivar* that he delivered his first hit. Soon thereafter, he was paired with a young Suchitra in *Sare Chuattor*, which became another big hit and popularised the 'Uttam and Suchitra' star pair. This success marked the beginning of the golden era of Bengali cinema. This romantic couple went on to star in a series of hit film, catapulting both to dizzy heights of success none had attained earlier in Bengali cinema.

Contrary to Suchitra's overpowering personality, Uttam was the quintessential man of the masses; literally the boy next door. The audience was totally taken up by his disarming charm. In most of his romantic roles, especially those starred with Suchitra, he was projected as the ideal male by both writers and directors. Uttam had acquired a certain image based on which scripts were being written. His filmmakers knew that any other image of Uttam besides that of a romantic hero could be a risk. Would an aggressive, go-getter image of Uttam have appealed to his fans? So while the *Mahanayak* was criticised for playing to the gallery, his romantic-hero image helped him secure a solid fan base, to experiment with other roles later in life, which his audience accepted without hesitation.

With over 200 films in Bengali cinema, Uttam had worked with most of the leading ladies of that era—Madhabi Mukherjee, Suchitra Sen, Supriya Devi, Mala Sinha, Sharmila Tagore and Aparna Sen. Describing his experience of working in romantic films and how he managed to deliver hit films with female stars, Uttam said, 'I pattern and redefine my romantic scenes according to the star I am cast with.' Elaborating on it, he said, 'When Arundhati Mukherjee was my leading lady, I tried to bring an intellectual flavour to my performance. I exercised restraint in the love scenes because Arundhati was herself quite controlled. With Sabitri, I was always on guard. She could beat me hollow in a scene without my knowing it.

She kept her senses totally alert in every shot. I have never seen an actress as powerful as Sabitri.'

Once Uttam achieved superstardom, he wearied of playing the same old lover-boy roles. His creative urge pushed him towards newer roles. Much of this experimentation might have also come about to prove his detractors wrong, especially those who thought he had limited calibre and could excel only in romantic roles.

During the early days, many intellectuals attacked Uttam for 'being theatrical and full of mannerisms'. He silenced them all with his sterling performances in films like *Nayak, Chowringee* (1968), *Anthony Firingi, Marutirtha Hinglaj* (1959), *Banpalashir Padabali* (1973), *Ananda Ashram* (1977), *Ogo Badgu Sundari* (1980) and *Iman Kalyan* (1981).

Uttam was the first Indian actor to recive the National Film Award for his outstanding performance in *Anthony Firingi* and *Chiriyakhana.* Predictably, his popularity with the masses did not impress the 'intellectuals' of Kolkata. Most detractors, however, were silenced once Satyajit Ray chose Uttam to work in *Nayak.* Working with Ray added a feather in Uttam's cap, starting an important phase in his life. Uttam was profoundly influenced by Ray.

Ray of course received flak from stalwarts of realistic cinema for using a popular hero in the role of *Nayak.* He said he had not written *Nayak* keeping Uttam in mind, but as the story unfolded, he could think of no one more suitable for the role that demanded both an actor and a star. 'Working with Uttam was a pleasant revelation,' Ray said, commenting on his dedication towards his work despite his *Mahanayak* status. He recounted how Uttam, instead of idling, would be quietly getting into the character of the film while waiting for the shots. In fact, he would ask relevant questions from time to time, which indicated his eagerness to mentally prepare for the role.

It was during this time that Uttam started experimenting with character roles and took on negative characters as well—perhaps, a deliberate attempt to break free from the stereotypical 'romantic hero' image he was stuck with, thanks to the pairing with Suchitra. Once Uttam gained the confidence to experiment with character roles, audience saw him essaying characters that were an interesting mix of good and bad. Critics often wonder what Uttam might have achieved had his talent been used for better and more diverse roles from the beginning.

Films like *Bicharak* (1959), *Jhinder Bondi* (1961), *Jatugriha* (1964) *Stree* (1972) and *Sanyasi Raja* (1975), with diverse roles and immaculate acting destroyed myths about his method acting, once and for all.

Be it as a villain or a comedian, serious or crazy, Uttam essayed each role with equal élan, earning much critical acclaim. The character of Chunilal, which he played in Dilip Roy's *Devdas,* is memorable for its freshness as well as spontaenity. In *Ayananta,* a film based on a novel by Samaresh Basu, he plays the villain obsessed with his love for a young woman with questionable morals. To his horror, when he discovers his love to be involved with his own friend, he kills her. Similarly, in the role of a cold-blooded, oppressive zamindar losing his sanity in *Lal Pathar* (1964) or as a middle-aged debauched man in *Bagh Bondi Khela* (1975), or, his sterling performances showcase an actor with a phenomenal range the audience never believed he had.

In an interview, he once mentioned that he faced his greatest challenge while doing the double role of two brothers in the film *Bhranti Bilas* (1963). Retaining the distinct identities of both roles was a formidable task. His performance in *Stree,* a film in which he plays the negligent husband caring little beyond his personal merriment and display of wealth, until he faces the truth about his wife fathering the son of another man, is astonishing. Similarly, his role of the guilty lawyer in *Bicharak* and the upright patriotic doctor in *Agniswar* (1975) are parts of the great body of work that Uttam has left behind.

In the age of black-and-white cinema, sans designer clothes, mind-blowing action or choreographed songs of today, characters were simple and far more demanding in terms of acting. Strangely, in the post-Uttam era, while Bengali cinema has gained in probably every department—technology, dance, lavish sets, bigger budgets and better costumes—it has still not been able to produce another Uttam.

If at times Uttam towered over everyone else in his brilliance, he could also take a backseat when required, allowing others to perform. Uttam was never quite as dramatic as Suchitra, and this very quality of being able to blend with the ethos of film made him indispensable.

Gopal Krishna Roy says, 'Despite the fact that I am close to Suchitra and have been her friend, in my personal opinion, Uttam is more versatile and diverse as an actor.' Whether it was practising lip-syncing or standing in front of the mirror and practising facial expressions, taking wrestling lessons from an *akhada* (wrestling ring) or learning to ride a horse, Uttam's dedication to a role has been exemplary. He used to keep a Mumbai *supari* (areca nut) in his mouth to be able to mouth dialogues for a longer time without being tired!

Once Salil Dutta came across Uttam on the sets of a film, but was surprised that the actor neither talked to nor acknowledged him, though both knew each other well! A disturbed Dutta shared this with an assistant on the sets. The assistant asked if Uttam was about to give a shot when Dutta met him. When Salil Dutta confirmed it, the assistant told him not to worry as Uttam was always preoccupied before giving a shot, lost in the character he was playing!

Uttam had a keen interest in the technicalities of filmmaking. Director Ajoy Kar says, 'Uttam, in his questions of the technical aspects of filmmaking, was much like a student of film studies. He would question me about camera and other technical aspects that go into filmmaking.'

Uttam impressed most people by his humility and adherence to perfection. However, his acceptance of his defects even when he was a *Mahanayak,* and his readiness to correct them endeared him to directors and producers. Tapan Sinha remembers that during the shooting of *Jhinder Bondi,* Uttam had told him, 'I am not very educated, Tapanda. My diction is not clear. So my dialogues sometimes sound forced. If at any time you find that I am unable to speak a given line in the manner you desire, please change it for my sake.' Tapan Sinha was moved by such humility. In another instance, when he was praised for his role in *Stree,* he attributed his success to Chhobi Biswas, his role model. Indeed, Uttam belonged to the rare breed of actors who had no qualms either about admitting to his shortcomings or acknowledging the influence of other actors on his work.

The government of West Bengal awarded him the best actor award in 1975.

In the mid-1950s, Uttam decided to venture beyond acting into the field of production. He co-produced his first film *Harano Sur* with director Ajoy Kar under the banner, Alochhaya Production Pvt Ltd. The film became a big hit and earned the Presidents' Regional Certificate of Merit Award in 1958. Soon Uttam turned a full-time producer with a number of hit films under the banner of his own production house, Uttam Films Pvt Ltd. The banner produced films like *Saptapadi, Bhranti Bilash, Uttar Phalguni, Grihadaha, Jatugriha* and *Chhoti Si Mulaqat.* All of these were hits except *Chhoti Si Mulaqat.* Uttam's direction of *Banpalashir Padabali* was also well-received. In a reflection of his excellence in this genre, the *Hindustan Standard* reported in its review on 16th February, 1978, 'In Uttam, we have found a director who shows his brilliance at diverse levels.'

Tapan Sinha, with whom he worked in *Jhinder Bondi* and *Jatugriha,* was impressed with him and said of the actor, 'He was a genius, though to survive, he had to make many films which did not appeal to him as an actor or a person.'

Most filmmakers and lovers of Bengali films will agree that no other actor in Bengal has been able to generate the kind of mass hysteria that Uttam did. Whenever Uttam made a public appearance, the crowd was unmanageable. Such was the hysteria of his fans that even during processions or peace marches in which he took part, he had to be placed in a lorry above everyone else so that the crowd could not reach him. Uttam himself rued the fact that he could not do many of the things he liked doing, such as visiting Durga Puja pandals or being a part of the Rather Mela in Kolkata after becoming a star.

The craze for Uttam is unflagging till today, and staple Bengali entertainment cannot do without one of *Mahanayak*'s films once in a while. That, perhaps, is the best reply to critics who didn't mince words with a man who never retaliated, even as a broken man in the end.

5

A Rare Chemistry

I seem to have loved you in numberless forms, numberless times...
In life, after life, in age, after age, forever.
My spellbound heart has made and remade the necklace of songs,
That you take as a gift, wear round your neck in your many forms,
In life, after life, in age, after age, forever.

Rabindranath Tagore

In 1993, *Baazigar* had most of us star-struck, with the intense display of passion by two relatively new faces—Shah Rukh Khan and Kajol. Their on-screen presence, their intense togetherness, their chemistry was so magical that the audience couldn't have asked for more! Both went on to become hugely popular in later years and acted with several other heroes and heroines. Yet, in spite of other hits with other actors, the rage and excitement these two generated together was incredible! Whether romancing each other or bickering, whenever they came together on the big screen, Shah Rukh and Kajol mesmerised their audience with the unmistakable stamp of being the perfect pair.

On-screen chemistry between two co-stars is usually a professional bond that succeeds in producing an undercurrent of intense camaraderie. Many are of the opinion that this chemistry can be established between two highly skilled artists, regardless of warm vibes or a great relationship off-screen. Yet others feel that great chemistry can be achieved only when two people share a special bond. Only when the actors are extremely comfortable in each other's presence can they pour their hearts into the roles, and emote effortlessly without any inhibition or restraint, while doing a intensely romantic scene.

Cinema history is replete with examples of screen pairings that have touched the hearts of millions. Famous off-screen pairs like Clark Gable-Vivien Leigh in *Gone with the Wind* (1939), Humphrey Bogart-Ingrid Bergman in *Casablanca* (1942), and closer home Raj Kapoor-Nargis reaffirm the fact that the chemistry between two filmstars creates absolute magic in a film and helps it become immensely popular.

In Bengali cinema, Uttam and Suchitra achieved the same magnitude of recognition. When they burst upon the scene as a pair in *Sare Chuattor*, little did they realise that it was the beginning of a tremendous pairing, in fact, the first ever in Bengali cinema.

What made Uttam and Suchitra an exceptional pair? Critics who put it down to their good looks and exceptional scripts need to re-evaluate their facile premises.

Before Uttam and Suchitra, there were several actors immensely good looking and talented as well. Yet there was no recognisable romantic pair that acquired a star-pair status. Kanan Devi (the first lady superstar of Bengal) and PC Barua were huge names and had a great fan following. Yet they were not considered a romantic pair despite having done a few films together.

When Uttam and Suchitra entered the industry, they too were paired with different actors. Uttam worked with many leading ladies like Manju De, Bharati Devi, Sandhya Rani, Sumitra Mukherjee, Sabitri Chatterjee and Supriya Devi—many of whom were exceptionally beautiful. Yet it was his work with Suchitra that left an undelible imprint on the minds of cinegoers. Suchitra, too, had worked with stalwarts like Basanta Chowdhury, Soumitra Chatterjee and Ranjit Mullick. However, the kind of adulation she achieved with Uttam was never repeated with any other hero, especially as far as romantic films were concerned.

To understand the success of this romantic pair, let's compare films of the previous generation with those of Uttam and Suchitra. Great actors like PC Barua and Kanan Devi would merge with their characters totally, without a hint of personal bearing. But in the case of Uttam and Suchitra, even when they immersed themselves in their characters, they managed to retain their individual magnetic presence. On-screen, they were as much the characters they played as Uttam and Suchitra, the glamorous stars. The sheer presence of the duo ensured that many nondescript scripts became instant hits.

What added to the romantic pairing were the excellent sets, the soft nuance of black-and-white films, haunting music and a dreamy air about the films. The pair was given meaningful dialogues amidst a setting and screenplay based on romantic literary pieces. Some stories transcended the boundaries of ordinary storytelling into something more ethereal and sublime, a hallmark of many Uttam and Suchitra films. Both passion and pathos were reflected through the pair and their cinematic tryst. Some memorable scenes that remain etched in the minds of viewers forever are of pain in intense love. Scenes like those in *Sagarika*, when Arun refuses to open his eyes after regaining his vision until he finds his Basanti (actually Sagarika), are heart-wrenching. Overwrought with emotions the audience cries with both Arun and Sagarika until they unite in a deep embrace. In *Kamallata*, when Kamal and Srikanto separate in the last scene at the railway station, their actions, though mature, is heartbreaking. Suchitra's lone tear drop, while the train pulls away out of the station, symbolises a thousand unspoken words that the lovers could not share. In *Shilpi*, when Dhiman dies and Anjana flings herself on him, screaming in agony, her loss resonates with the viewers in rural Bengal who lost their loved ones to famine or flood.

Uttam's and Suchitra's celluloid escapades left the palate for romance craving for more. From brooding to mellow, they covered the entire repertoire. However, much of Uttam's and Suchitra's craze had to do with a society that was still awkward with issues of romance and intimacy. The socio-cultural milieu of the 1950s, when the pair reigned as screen idols, prohibited of public expression of love. Uttam and Suchitra broke that taboo. Be it by gazing at each other forlornly or by singing songs hand in hand, and other romantic intimacies, they chose to explore unchartered territory.

Uttam and Suchitra singing songs together or going on a date by the hills, as in *Agniparikhsha*, were beyond the imagination of the common man. Scenes where they were shown to be intimate, stoked longing in young minds. In many ways, Uttam and Suchitra represented what young lovers sought from their love lives, but could not attain. They would often, clandestinely, watch an Uttam and Suchitra film and derive vicarious pleasure from it.

Yet Uttam and Suchitra films were never vulgar or gross. They were glamorous and titillating, yet full of substance; deeply passionate, yet serenely sublime. At a day and age when sleaze is the criteria for popularity it is surprising to see that Uttam and Suchitra films, which dared to defy social conventions, yet maintained the fine balance of elegance and passion, are still so popular.

A recent pair Prosenjit and Rituparna is a bigger money-spinner in the Bengali film industry. But none have measured up to the wonderful togetherness of Uttam and Suchitra.

By a time when the magic names 'Uttam and Suchitra' spelt box-office success, filmmakers had started showing scenes of physical intimacy. This trend, in fact, started with *Agniparikhsha* when Uttam and Suchitra were first seen embracing each other. After the stupendous success of this film, directors would include one climactic scene where the hero and the heroine would be standing at a distance from each other, looking passionately at each other, with unshed tears in their eyes, and suddenly, to perfect timing, they would run towards each other and embrace! Indeed what's an Uttam and Suchitra film without those coy glances, intense looks and that lasting embrace.

There were, of course, other such scenes meant to titillate the youth and a romance-starved generation. The touching of hands, close-ups of their faces together, and many love-lorn looks that the couple exchanged, were all part of the romantic fervour that Uttam and Suchitra rustled up.

In *Ekti Raat* (1956), the story of a couple spending a night together in spite of being married to other people, Uttam and Suchitra are shown sharing a bed for the night. Though the film borders on the comic, scenes where a writhing Suchitra is shown in bed with Uttam expressing his wish to spend more time with her, are examples of a romance that the audience simply lapped up. The Uttam and Suchitra charisma apart and how adorable they looked together, the love scripted by them highlighted their charm. Both had a happy-go-lucky air about them and a certain youthfulness that was refreshingly appealing.

With the exception of *Shilpi*, which shows Uttam dying, the biggest selling point of an Uttam and Suchitra hit was to follow the same romantic formula. In an interview to Gaurango Prasad Ghosh, Uttam narrated an amusing anecdote on how this demand would influence even a serious script. During the shooting of *Saptapadi*, it had been decided that the film would end with the heroine dying on the beach and her lover pining for her. On hearing this, the producer approached Uttam with folded hands and pleaded, 'Please do not show a tragic end with the death of Suchitra, the heroine. We will be deprived of a hit film and ruined by financial debts.' According to him the audience would have never accepted a film where Uttam and Suchitra were not united at the end. He even suggested an appropriate ending where the heroine could emerge from the sea and fling herself on the hero. Highly amused, Uttam asked the producer to meet scriptwriter, Nitai Bhattacharya, with a request for the necessary changes. Nitai Bhattacharya apparently demanded a princely sum of ₹ 2,000 to do so. *Saptapadi* ended on an ambiguous note. The last scene showed Uttam carrying Suchitra amidst tall shadows of a church, indicating a holy union. Scriptwriter Bhattacharya had obviously made a smart move. By allowing the audience to decide their own end, he managed to satisfy his producer, and retain the artistic sensibility of a serious script.

Despite great scripts and equally good music, the credit of bringing in a certain stylised artistic flair to acting must be attributed to Uttam and Suchitra. Like Uttam, Suchitra, too, fit into every role with ease. Be it a haughty Rina Brown, a docile Kamallata or a self-sacrificing Sagarika, she was both glamour personified and a reigning queen of passion, melting into great acting with such finesse that she was often compared to no less than Meena Kumari.

Contrary to what Suchitra showcased in many of her films, women had not forayed out to work for a living those days. In fact, women were rarely seen alone or unaccompanied on the streets. Suchitra, with her glamour and sophistication, became the idol for not only men but also women who wanted to emulate her in everyway. With her behaviour and her empowered state, she became an unparalleled icon for a whole new generation. Questions about her acting abilities were virtually ignored. Uttam, on his part was manna from heaven—not only a perfect foil to Suchitra's histrionics but also the producer's ticket to financial success.

However, in most Uttam and Suchitra films, there was precious little experimentation with them as a pair. Uttam usually played the role of either a spoilt and egoistic male or that of a rustic and ignored plebeian who had to be raised in social status by the rich and affluent Suchitra as his partner in love. Suchitra was mostly portrayed as the quintessential woman—rich or poor, someone who was amazingly good at almost everything.

There were of course exceptions to the rule, but in general, a confused Uttam seeking to rise above every obstacle in life by surrendering to his love was a theme that the audience seemed to love. This was emblematic of the social conditions of that time. In most cases, the duo was shown romancing without the permission of their parents. Suchitra was usually shown as a girl from a well-off family, while Uttam belonged to a poor family. All disapproval was surmounted by the couple, who found bliss in each other's arms by the end of the film.

Clichéd as it may sound, the pair probably traversed every difficult road that one would imagine impeding lovers. In *Har Mana Har*, when Nira comes to seek Binu's blessings on passing her exams, he plucks a flower from the vase and pins it on her hair, saying, '*Ami shilpi, chobi enke debo bolechhilam, phool diye sajiye dilam. Khub sundor dekhachhe, ainay nijer chhobi ta dekho, mone hobe amar anka chhobi tai pran peyeche*' (I am an artist, I had told you that I would give you a painting, but could not. But now the picture is complete. You look beautiful, look at yourself in the mirror, it would seem as if my painting has been given a life).

Such romance was poetry on celluloid. Whether it was romance that bloomed amidst problems as in *Shilpi*, the sense of purity that lovers share in *Kamallata*, the austerity and sacrifice in *Grihadaha* or the sublime Rina Brown and Krishnendu in *Saptapadi*, Uttam and Suchitra played their romance with such precision that few could imagine one without the other.

Critics have often commented on the seemingly patterned romances of Uttam and Suchitra. Whether one calls it playing to the gallery or the audience's limited vision of the way in which they wanted to see Uttam and Suchitra, the fact remains that the pair had to serve up what the public demanded. An Uttam and Suchitra film that broke many such patterns was *Nabarag* (1971). Here, Suchitra was shown as belonging to a poor family and the rich and aristocratic Uttam takes a fancy to her. The film has plenty of scenes which would have shocked the audience of those times: Suchitra in the shower, or baring her legs partially on the beach or even indulging in social drinking—a departure from the couple's other films.

Uttam and Suchitra were also perfect foils to each other. Suchitra was usually a lady with an ego and blistering personality, while Uttam was the affable lover with a touch of mischievousness, with a song on his lips, and his winsome smile. Suchitra's haughty demeanour, where she was shown belonging to a rich family, looked very real. On the other hand, Uttam's gullible disposition and charm made him the perfect lover who would ultimately win over his lady love. Together, they were a pair pitted as opposites that attract, yet they had inherent similarities

Beginning with *Sare Chuattor*, Uttam and Suchitra worked in 30 films. While *Agnipariksha* and *Saptapadi* are regarded as milestones in their careers, *Sagarika* was a huge hit and ran for more than six months in some theatres. Everything they did together sold. Perhaps, that is why both Uttam and Suchitra were also roped into the marketing processes of the films as well. The posters of *Sagarika* had a line from the actors themselves: 'In a romantic portrayal, in our performance together, Sagarika will remain memorable.' Below this line were the signatures of Uttam and Suchitra.

In Gopal Krishna Roy's book, Suchitra says, 'In order to form this romantic pair, a lot of knots had to be opened,' revealing little-known tribulations that came in the way of establishing the Uttam and Suchitra pair. Initially there may have been vested interests, within the industry, working against casting the two together, but there were other snags as well.

Uttam and Suchitra had to fight an uphill battle against a section of cinegoers in Kolkata—highbrowed intellectuals rejected romantic films altogether. These educated Bengalis, steeped in nationalistic sentiments with strong political affiliations, preferred theatre, instead. To them, Gulam Khuddus's recitation or Tulsi Lahiri's theatre was far more alluring.

Others were those drawn to Hindi cinema. This group was the lot affected by the tumult of Partition, easily given to the escapism and glamour of Hindi films. Popular Hindi cinema pairs, such as Ashok Kumar and Devika Rani or Raj Kapoor and Nargis reigned supreme in their hearts, with little scope for Bengali artists to claim a share of the pie.

Given the situation, it was left to Uttam and Suchitra to not only revive interest in Bengali cinema but also to offer the audience what they wanted: romance, glamour and a feel-good factor that stayed with them after they walked out of the theatres. In hindsight, one might conclude that the initial magnetism of a fresh good-looking pair, with intense chemistry was an immediate crowd puller, which later on settled down to acknowledging their acting capabilities as well. It was with this gradual realisation that Uttam and Suchitra's films were in fact a rare combination of good and passionate cinema, that things began changing for the better.

However much Uttam and Suchitra maintained that they were nothing but colleagues, their fans perceived them as a couple. Most believed that without a strong mutual attraction, the passion and romance portrayed by them on-screen, would not be possible.

The Uttam and Suchitra craze dominated Bengali cinema at a time when Uttam worked with several other leading ladies. While gossip on affairs between heroes and heroines is commonplace today, oftentimes, cultivated as a part of a film's promotional pitch, Uttam and Suchitra needed no such fad to fuel their popularity. For one, neither bothered to hide his/her marital status and more surprisingly, the Uttam and Suchitra romance story stood its ground despite the fact that everyone knew that Uttam was involved with Supriya Devi.

With her moving expressions, dynamic screen presence, beautiful face, magnificent smile and intelligent yet haughty air, Suchitra was what male fantasy was made of. Uttam, on the other hand, seemed the epitome of a desirable man: handsome yet sensitive, proud yet vulnerable in love, with a smile that set female hearts aflutter.

Much of the Uttam and Suchitra off-screen romance could have been pure conjecture but it is also possible that the truth was never allowed to surface. Love outside marriage was still a taboo; added to it was a societal notion of a virtuous woman—limited to the roles of mother, wife or sister but never a lover. That Suchitra was a married woman was never forgotten. Had Uttam and Suchitra made any public display of emotions, it would have had a disastrous impact on their lives and careers. As professionals and as individuals, Uttam and Suchitra were very aware of their image and status.

Yet, however much Uttam and Suchitra tried to retain their privacy, they were inexplicably linked together in the imagination of their fans and by the press. Local magazines circulated stories about their off-screen romance, even when neither of them bothered to either deny or confirm these rumours. That Suchitra was passing through troubled times in her marriage might have added grist to the mill. According to studio gossip, Uttam had proposed to Suchitra several times, but she did not accept his proposal since she believed in the sanctity of marriage and was aware of her standing in society.

The playful side to their relationship clearly visible and indicative of a special chemistry didn't help quell rumours either. Uttam was one of the few people who had the privilege of calling Suchitra by her real name—Roma. They also endearingly addressed each other as '*tui*' (equivalent of Hindi '*tu*'; used only with very close relationships in Bengali).

Apparently Suchitra, who called herself Uttam's *Priyo Bandhobi*, would often visit him both at home and in the studios. Like lovers they would bicker with each other about their roles, have tiffs both dramatic and personal, and even cajole each other into doing things that others could never make them do. Co-actors, technicians and directors, gossiped about the close relationship that blossomed between Uttam and Suchitra

The two were known to constantly keep each other company in their make-up vans. In fact, many studio hands spoke of how the two went out for drives together if they were shooting in adjacent locations. Visiting each other on the sets or sharing food between shots was also quite commonplace. Platonic or spiritual, their mutual admiration was palpable and infectious. Both shared much more than their films and would even look to each other for solace in times both good and bad.

While reading interviews of Uttam or watching his little habits, one finds an astonishing influence of Suchitra. Perhaps, over the years, they imbibed some of each other's traits. While it is known to most that Suchitra visited the Belur Math, few know that Uttam did so, too. Both of them would religiously sit in their puja rooms in the morning, and loved incense sticks. What brought them together, however, was their common passion for excellence in cinema, the thirst for making it big and the will to fight their way to the top. This is perceptible in their choice of scripts which matured over time, and their acting in terms of emoting and dialogue delivery which became less theatrical and more subtle. The two had tremendous respect for each other, too. Uttam's and Suchitra's relationship was based on mutual trust, appreciation and admiration for each other's work and personality.

An anecdote goes that during the shooting of *Priyo Bandhobi,* Suchitra had arrived on time for the shoot but Uttam was late. While she waited in her make-up van, Suchitra enquired about the delay. Upon learning that the shooting was held up because of Uttam, she informed the producer that she would wait for only five minutes more. If Uttam did not turn up by that time, she would leave; and she left, as threatened.

When Uttam arrived on the sets, and learnt that Suchitra had left, being an astute man he got the message. Suchitra purportedly called the producer later and told him that whatever she had done was for the best and that he should deduct his losses for the day from her fees. True to her estimation, thereafter, Uttam was always on time for all the other shots of the film.

Suchitra's influence on Uttam and vice-versa was well known to most in the industry. For the shooting of *Priyo Bandhobi,* Uttam could allot only few dates at first. When the perturbed producer contacted Suchitra, she took the responsibility of talking to Uttam; the matter was resolved in no time with the producer being allotted adequate dates. Similarly, on several occasions, when Suchitra, famous for her tantrums, refused to shoot, Uttam cajoled her into relenting. The fact that she had to always be cajoled by Uttam also fuelled the curiosity of bystanders who vouched they had a special relationship.

Perhaps, it is this influence which led Uttam to seek her out in moments of crisis, too. Hushed rumours suggest that on the evening of 3rd September, 1963 during a celebration in his house, Uttam had gone upstairs to receive a call from Supriya Devi. A suspicious Gauri Devi followed her husband and a big fight ensued between the two. Uttam left his home that night, following months of tension between them. While it was reported that Uttam had gone to Supriya Devi's Moira Street home, the fact was that he had actually first gone to Suchitra's home. But Suchitra could not take him in because of her own problems.

Photographer Dhiren Deb recalls an occasion when he photographed the pair in a carefree mood. At the Bengal Film Journalist Association's annual prize distribution ceremony, while plenty of photographers happily clicked away the closely seated Uttam and Suchitra, Dhiren Deb waited for his moment. He observed Uttam and Suchitra deep in conversation. His instinct told him he might be able to capture a special moment. With luck on his side, he clicked one of the most memorable pictures that captured the duo's beautiful chemistry. A laughing Suchitra and a happy Uttam winking at her made it to the front page of *Cine Advance*. To thousands of Uttam and Suchitra fans, the photograph spoke volumes about their favourite off-screen affection.

When a rumour-mongering magazine once reported that Suchitra brought special lunch for Uttam, during their shooting, Uttam immediately announced that in order to respect public sentiments, Suchitra would have to do exactly so. While this caused much amusement amongst the duo and their colleagues, it is a marker of the collective thought of a generation who refused to accept Uttam without Suchitra, either in reality or in films.

Despite rumours of their blossoming closeness, it is, however, quite possible they were much ahead of their times, sharing a unique friendship not in accordance with social conventions. Tarun Kumar, Uttam's brother agrees that, 'The very modernity of their relationship might have courted controversies. After all, one must remember those were times when society was yet to acknowledge close friendship between a man and a woman.'

When actress Madhabi Mukherjee was asked to comment on what she thought about their romantic relationship off-screen, she replied, 'Uttam and Suchitra shared a beautiful relationship. Such cannot be seen today.' She added, 'They had tremendous respect for each other's work and all of us co-actors would love to think they had something between them.' But even she believes that their on-screen performance would not have been as brilliant had they been involved.

Supriya Devi, Uttam's companion of 17 years, narrates several incidents that bring to light another dimension of this friendship. Passionate romance or teasing humour, Suchitra is believed to have pulled Supriya's leg on many such occasions. Once, when Suchitra called up to speak to Uttam, on being informed that he had stepped out, she mischievously added, 'What a pity. I felt like kissing him.'

Again, during the shooting of *Priyo Bandhobi*, Suchitra played a prank, quite uncharacteristic of her reserved self. On realising that Supriya was visiting the sets, she suddenly embraced Uttam and asked Supriya Devi, 'Are you jealous?' To which Supriya Devi replied how accustomed even she was to the Uttam and Suchitra craze and hence not jealous at all.

During the shooting of *Har Mana Har* in Chandipur, Supriya recalls Uttam and Suchitra had arranged for a party in the evening, after the shooting. When Supriya Devi reached the party, she had found Uttam and Suchitra sitting together. During the party, the couple also enjoyed a dance together, and a teasing Suchitra didn't fail to enquire again and again if Supriya was envious that she was with her man.

Amidst affection and spontaneity, there were also ego clashes which often took a serious turn, bringing the shooting to a halt. Director Hari Das Babu once commented, 'Whenever Uttam and Suchitra would shoot together, there would be some problem or the other. Whether it was to do with dialogues or a particular pose they did not like, they would simply stall the shooting.'

There were also rumours about misunderstandings between the two great artistes. This was once brought to the fore, during the shooting of *Pothe Holo Deri*. The shooting was in Darjeeling and both Uttam and Suchitra were staying in the hotel. A friend of Uttam's had clicked a photograph of Suchitra without seeking her permission. This irritated Suchitra who was quick to show her disapproval. Though the photographer destroyed the film in front of her, the matter was reported to Uttam, who on his part, objected to Suchitra's husband Dibanath Sen bringing a camera to the shoot of the

film, the next day. Uttam objected to the presence of Mr Sen, saying that he was being disturbed by the outsider's presence. This created tension between the stars and shooting was stalled. Suchitra was miffed at her husband being insulted. It took much convincing to get the two stars back to the shoot and finally all was well again and the film went on to become a major hit, running for 11 weeks in Kolkata.

Gopal Krishna Roy says whenever he tried to ask Suchitra about her relationship with Uttam, she either clammed up or got into a philosophical mood. It would be impossible to extract a proper reply from her. 'When I told her once that there was a particular look she had for Uttam, which was distinctly different from what she had for other heroes, she ignored the fact and went on to say that on the sets, they were nothing but extreme professionals. What they were outside the sets, therefore, remain a matter of much speculation.'

When asked what he thought made the couple so special, he replied 'As a romantic pair, they were simply superb. It is my personal opinion that there are many artistes who can show a love affair on-screen, but what Uttam and Suchitra projected was beyond that of a normal love affair; it was a sort of meeting of two perfect souls who did not only complement each other physically but also shared a strong bond that was platonic as much as it was romantic. Their emotional-spiritual bonding made the pairing so special.'

Suchitra had once revealed that the first time she met Uttam on the sets of the film *Sare Chuattor*, she was very impressed by him. At that time, Uttam was already a known face and she had great admiration for his work. The two of them were introduced to each other by their director Nirmal Dey with whom they worked together for the next 23 years.

Amidst gossip about them in the Kolkata social circuit, Uttam and Suchitra maintained a dignified presence in public. When asked about the pair's intensity, Suchitra had once replied, 'When Uttam and I were on the floor for a shot, we ceased to be our personal selves; the characters we played took over.'

Interestingly, whenever Suchitra was asked to define her relationship with Uttam, she was brief with her words. She would usually dismiss it as 'just friends'. Uttam admitted to having not only a soft corner for Suchitra, but also that he was in awe of her as a co-actor, as well as a person. Uttam replied, 'Yes I loved her, but this love is of a different kind and genre.' He reportedly once said that the fact that Suchitra was such an attractive woman spurred his acting abilities and made it easier for him to emote as an actor, too. He apparently admitted that while acting with Suchitra, he looked forward to the romance, unlike his earlier heroines who were mostly much older to him. In an interview with Ranjan Bandopadhay, Uttam said, 'Roma is the most beautiful, the most glamorous among all my leading ladies. I have been lucky to have had the exclusive right to be cast as the man she falls in love with.'

Whether Suchitra had the same feelings for him was endlessly discussed in drawing rooms. It was neither validated nor denied by Suchitra. Yet she had once said, 'I don't care about other actors, but Uttam is very special. I have never seen a great actor like him.'

Contrary to Suchitra's stoic silence about their relationship, Uttam was quite forthcoming about Suchitra's influence on him, 'While working in the film *Sare Chuattor* with Roma, I understood that my heroine had arrived. Had Suchitra not been by my side, I would never have been Uttam.' Humbling words indeed from a star as great as him, but that was the hallmark of a man who had genuine adulation for his co-star.

Uttam had, at various stages, shown his gratitude to director Nirmal Dey for casting him with Suchitra. He had once said that his career would have been over had it not been for the legendary pairing which came about just at the right time. Uttam had further elaborated that in films like *Agnipariksha* and *Sagarika*, their glamour had been well utilised. He had also commented on the fact that often filmmakers would ask Suchitra and him to act or pose in a particular way, but that they would try to enact it to the best of their capabilities, trying to make it appear as natural as possible. Once when Uttam was asked by his biographer Gaurango Prasad Ghosh about the preference being given to Suchitra's name in the posters or even in the introduction of the films, Uttam had replied that Roma had given him preference as a hero above all others male actors, and that was more than sufficient for him.

The more one watches Uttam and Suchitra films, the more one realises how good they were together. The scene in *Saptapadi*, where Rina Brown packs Krishnendu's bags, or the scene where Krishnendu and Rina Brown ride a bike into eternity or even the funny sight of Rampriti following Romola on the roads in *Sare Chuattor* shall stay with the audience forever. In *Sagarika*, when Arun calls out in anguish for his Sagar after his operation and says he does not want to live in a world of light without her because she is his light, it seems real. In *Kamallata*, when Srikanto asks Kamal when he should be leaving the ashram, 'Perhaps never,' replies a determined Kamal—which is heartrending.

Such was the elegance and poise of the Uttam and Suchitra pairing that several years later, the magic is still alive. Indeed Uttam and Suchitra on celluloid seemed to overshadow everything, including their individual selves.

Whether Uttam and Suchitra were as deeply involved with each other in reality shall forever remain unanswered. Gopal Krishna Roy says, 'Suchitra had visited Uttam on his last journey, on the day of his death at 2:30 at night. When the garland that she had brought along with her was placed on the body of Uttam, she whispered, "Gently lest he be hurt." '

6

Memorable Films and Scenes

Only I have heard his gentle footsteps from the road before my house.
The livelong day has passed in spreading his seat on the floor;
But the lamp has not been lit and I cannot ask him into my house.
I live in the hope of meeting with him; but this meeting is not yet.

Rabindranath Tagore

Uttam and Suchitra worked in 30 films together. Some of the films and scenes are classics today, not for any technical reasons but purely due to their popularity. These films not only bear testimony to the changes in society, culture, values and the literature of the time, they also provide us with a glimpse of the off-screen bond between Uttam and Suchitra. Through this journey, from their first film to their last, one observes their emerging technical understanding and their development as keen artistes. Their choice of films indicates an undeniable and increasingly mature rapport between the two.

Going beyond critical acclaim, some of these films and scenes immediately come to mind, each time Uttam and Suchitra are mentioned.

Agnipariksha

Agnipariksha is an interesting tale that delves into the traditional ritual of child marriage and revolves around its impact on the protagonists, who, like the society itself, are caught at a crossroad full of dilemmas, in their attempt to break away from traditions and embrace modernity.

Bulu and Tapasi, married as children, grow up in two different environments. Tapasi's mother urges her to forget the marriage and move on in life in keeping with her elite urbane upbringing. Consequently, Tapasi as an adult bumps into a stranger, Kiriti, with whom she falls in love. The stranger is none other than Bulu, her child-groom who has also set out to see if their marriage vows, taken as children, mean anything at all. Unaware of the unfolding drama around her, Tapasi continues to remain tormented by her past. When, as a couple Kiriti and Tapasi try to reach a conclusive decision, Tapasi is unable to break away from traditions. She decides to forgo her love to remain true to her sacred vows. She returns to the village in search of Bulu only to find, to her great surprise and relief, that Bulu and Kiriti are one and the same.

This film directed by Agradoot, and produced by Uttam himself, was probably one of the most important films by Uttam and Suchitra that propelled them to stardom. The film also confirmed Suchitra's great acting ability and elevated her status in the Bengali film industry. *Agnipariksha* was also memorable as a film that dispelled the cloud of gloom that had been hanging over the Bengali film industry for some time. It became a huge commercial success, blurring the divide between commercial and art cinema.

The film is both intense and sensitive in the fine portrayal of characters by Uttam and Suchitra. The depiction of Tapasi's inner turmoil, resulting from her inability to come to terms with sacrificing her love for tradition, is intense. Though understated, Suchita's expressions speak of an actress of calibre. The director's handling of the script, showing the conflict between traditional beliefs and the need for inner transformation, is deft and sensitive. The music and the lyrics of the songs are well suited to giving vent to Tapasi's suppressed emotion.

Agnipariksha is also a social commentary on Kolkata's Westernised upper class and their elite education, embodied by Loretto School and The Presidency, in the film. It also raises issues, such as child marriage and its impact on children, traditional Bengali social values and the premium set on money over relationships.

In several scenes in the film, Uttam and Suchitra emote in the most sensuous manner. The scene in which Bulu and Tapasi first meet is unusually novel; atop a mountain, both are trapped in fog and must spend a few hours together. Tapasi, a singer enthralls Kiriti as well as the audience, with her soulful singing. In an outburst of emotion, when Tapasi suddenly visits Kiriti's home, the audience is as captivated as the hero. When Kiriti accidentally touches her and expresses remorse at his action, Suchitra's poignant song '*Jodi Bhul Kore*' communicates her ecstacy to the audience as well. On the day of their engagement, when Tapasi and Kiriti confess their love, not so much in words as through action, the viewers experience their inner turmoil coming in the way of their love.

Suchitra is beautiful in a saree worn in the traditional Bengali style and Uttam looks dapper in suits, portraying the part of the '*Bilet ferot*' (foreign returned) much-in-demand zamindar bachelor boy. Be it because of songs like '*Gane More*' or '*Jodi Bhul Kore*' or the chemistry between Uttam and Suchitra, *Agnipariksha* will always remain a very special film in this star-pair's career graph.

Sare Chuattor

Sare Chuattor is a comedy around the unexpected arrival of a young girl, Romola, with her parents, at a male boarding house. She becomes the focus of unrivalled attention with each boy in the premises trying to woo her in his own special way. Finally the suave Rampriti wins her heart after a rollercoaster ride of misunderstandings that ends in mutual admiration and matrimony. Amusingly, all the boys who wooed her join in happily in the celebrations, conveying the simplicity of those times. Misunderstandings between Rajanibabu (veteran actor Tulsi Chakkraborty), who acts as an emissary between the lovers, and his wife, over misplaced love-notes lead to some of the most hilarious scenes of the film. Tulsi Chakraborty's fine acting and over-the-top reactions make it a light-hearted fare, for everyone to enjoy.

It was the youth, however, that identified with the film immediately, when it was released. Scenes with each boarding-house boy trying his luck with Romola are fabulous. The internal petty politics and the competition for winning a look from Romola are hilariously depicted. Set in the fun-filled ambience of a male boarding house, the viewers are treated to the activities that make up the life of the boys; their daily routine and their boisterous rib-tickling fun, making for a youthful and vibrant experience.

The cast of *Sare Chuattor* became bigger than the film itself. A hit when it was released in 1953, the film is today remembered for bringing together the eternal romantic pair Uttam and Suchitra. A laugh riot, it had several other great artists besides Uttam and Suchitra. Tulsi Chakraborty and Bhanu Banerjee's roles were outstanding.

Made at a time when both Uttam and Suchitra were struggling to make it big as actors, the film lacks the finesse of their future films. Nevertheless, Uttam and Suchitra became the biggest crowd-puller. Scenes where Uttam and Suchitra are shown at loggerheads with each other were lapped up by the audience for the tension they managed to create. As in most Uttam and Suchitra films, Rampriti seems to be in awe of Romola and a tad confused about the right way of handling her. The scenes where he follows his lady love around town and tries his hand at wooing her are a perfect blend of farce and romance.

The comedy is heightened by the presence of the boys from the hostel who form curious onlookers.

Harano Sur

Harano Sur is about the life of a patient Alok Mukherjee, who suffers from temporary loss of memory after a train accident. Dr Roma Banerjee rescues him and takes him to her father's (Pahari Sanyal) country house in a village called Palaspur to treat him. Here they fall in love and marry but a second accident makes him recall his life as a rich businessman in Kolkata and he forgets Roma altogether. More intrigue ensues with Roma taking up a job in the Mukherjee household as a governess to try and restore Alok's memory. Much heartbreak later when Alok follows Roma to Palspur, he gradually realises the truth. The journey to recover their lost love ends with the *Harano Sur* (lost melody) restored to their lives. The repetition of the score '*Tumi Je Amar*', throughout the film is an attempt at reminding Alok of yesteryears.

Like all Uttam and Suchitra films, other characters have also played important roles. Utpal Dutt, in a brief but stellar performance makes an impact, as does Pahari Sanyal, as Roma's father.

Harano Sur is replete with intense love scenes between Alok and Roma. But this romance does not lie in just dialogue and the presence of Uttam and Suchitra in every frame. The romantic and sensitive ambience, with gestures like Alok pinning a flower on Roma's hair, or Roma putting him to sleep, or Roma knitting a sweater for Alok or being totally shattered when he suddenly vanishes from Palashpur, are memorable. Alok's total surrender to his doctor, his childlike dependence on her, is also touching. The scenes of Alok and Roma gradually falling in love are subtle and tender, created so artistically that they leaves the viewer craving for more. Another memorable romantic scene is that of their marriage, where a resplendent Roma in her bridal finery sings for the first time '*Tumi Je Amar*', while Alok enjoys every bit of the loving caresses in her lap. The melodious voice of Geeta Dutt in this song and the magic of the Uttam and Suchitra romance shall haunt the audience for decades to come.

The scene where Roma visits Alok, the businessman, and realises that he does not recognise her is poignant with the emotional trauma of a forgotten wife. Her pained expression where she tells Alok, now her employer, that she is 'no one but a governess', and that 'her husband has forgotten her', haunts the viewers. The film reaches a high point of drama and romantic tension when a desperate Roma tells Alok, '*Jodi boli apnakei khujchhi*' (If I say I was searching for you). A visibly disturbed Alok and a desparate Roma bring much depth into these scenes where the battle to regain not only the lost melody *(Harano Sur)* but also all those memories that matter the most, is not only fought quietly but eventually won.

Shilpi

Shilpi is one of the most popular films of Uttam and Suchitra. Made in 1956 by the Agranami Group, *Shilpi,* is a romantic tragedy and adds another dimension to the Uttam and Suchitra repertoire. The film, unlike any Uttam and Suchitra starrer, had the audience weep along with them in their quest for love. *Shilpi* is the story of an artist Dhiman and his love for his muse Anjana. It is a commentary on the prevalent zamindari system and the discrimination against those who belong to the working class. A young Dhiman is given a roof over his head and coached by the best of artists, thanks to the arrogant zamindar who happens to be Anjana's father. In a creative atmosphere, young Dhiman and Anjana are drawn to each other. Dhiman shows great promise as an artist and is encouraged in his creative pursuits by his teachers and Anjana herself. As the two grow up, they fall in love. Predictably, most members of the family oppose their relationship, especially Anjana's father who wants her to marry the son of a wealthy friend. Amid threats from the zamindar and insults by Anjana (who is forced to do so by her father), Dhiman goes back to his poverty-stricken village. The latter half of the film is a commentary of sorts on famine-stricken rural Bengal juxtaposed with the opulence of the zamindari lifestyle. It is here that a frustrated and desolate Dhiman, nursing the lament of a lost love, breathes his last, while a frustrated Anjana languishes in futile protest.

Though theatrical in its approach, *Shilpi* sees some fine acting by Uttam. His sensitive portrayal of Dhiman and the knowledge of the pointlessness of his position are remarkable. Anjana is portrayed as a pretty young thing in the first half; her depth is brought out through the tragedy she faces in the latter half.

The romantic scenes in *Shilpi* aesthetically depict the mutual love, respect and admiration that the lovers feel as artist and muse. Symbolism plays a big role throughout. Dhiman's suffering is picturised very well initially through his paintings, and later through the gradual deterioration of his body.

The suffering of the separated lovers, especially the scene where Anjana sings in front of her fiancé while her mind and heart are with Dhiman, are agonising. Dhiman and Anjana defy parental strictures, to meet each other, something that must have shocked the audience of those times. On an outing, when a beautiful Anjana lying on the ground whispers sweet nothings to a happy Dhiman, the audience is transported to another world. Be it in scenes of sweet love or in the pathos of lovers languishing for each other in *Shilpi,* the world of art and creation are intermingled with that of love. Dhiman, who had worked on beauty only through his brush for long, now, faces the reality of having lost his beloved. Consequently, his art tinged with humility and pain, scales great heights.

Like all other Uttam and Suchitra films, music is the major attraction in *Shilpi.* The sound of *shehnai* (a wind instrument), usually associated with marriage as well as the *bidai* (a bride's departure from her parental abode), is skillfully used in the background to accentuate the pain of the separated lovers.

Indrani

Indrani, directed by Niren Lahiri in 1958, was one of the biggest blockbusters from the hit pair. The film shows Indrani's journey and the agonising ramifications of her transformation from a young college girl to a powerful woman. Like many other Uttam and Suchitra films, this one, too, comes with a message and comment on social evils. The link between money and social status is brought to the fore, when Indrani, an assistant headmistress, grows in status while her unemployed husband Sudarshan struggles to keep up with her. She nearly loses him in the process. But Sudarshan is propelled into limelight for his work. Realising the emptiness of her life without him, Indrani rushes back to her husband. The ego clashes between a jobless husband and his powerful wife have been handled with great efficacy. Also noteworthy are the scenes depicting social hypocrisies.

As always, the chemistry between Uttam and Suchitra be it in the girls' hostel or at sunset, compensates for the pitfalls in the film. One of the most unforgettable scenes in the film is where the couple is having an argument when Sudarshan stops to just stare at Indrani for a long time. When Indrani asks him what he is searching, he says, *'Indrani ke, je hariye ghechhe'* (I am searching for the Indrani, who is lost). *Indrani* is also replete with beautiful songs. Each song is remembered for the immense beauty of its picturisation and its melody. Three of the songs,

'*Nir Chhoto Khoti Nei*', '*Jhanak Jhanak*' and '*Surjo Dobar Pala*' have been all-time hits. '*Nir Chhoto Khoti Nei*', a duet that Indrani and Sudarshan sing in their new home, in Hemanta Kumar and Geeta Dutt's voices, marks the coming together of two kindred souls. Interestingly, the film also has a Hindi song, '*Sabh Kuchh Lutakar*', which is both prophetic and inspiring.

Saptapadi

Saptapadi is probably the only Uttam and Suchitra film that has something for everyone. One of their finest films, it remains a favourite with most Bengali cinegoers even today. Directed by Ajoy Kar, the film is set against the backdrop of World War II. It opens with the revered Krishnendu, a doctor who runs a military hospital in Bankura. His daily routine is disrupted by the arrival of a drunken Anglo-Indian woman soldier who jolts him out of his reverie and takes the story back in time, when Krishnendu and Rina Brown were medical college students. Amid the regular rich girl-poor boy ego clashes, the two fall in love. In accordance with Rina's father's wishes, Krishnendu readily agrees to convert to Christianity, but the love story is interrupted by Krishnendu's father (Chhobi Biswas) who comes in the way, and extracts a promise from Rina to convert to Hinduism. A shattered Rina gets Krishnendu out of her life and the two meet many years later in a war-torn area. Misunderstandings are set straight by a letter from Krishnendu's father and at last, Rina and Krishnendu reunite against the backdrop of war.

Saptapadi has immensely popular song '*Ei Poth Jodi Na Shesh Hoy.*' Ajoy Kar's direction is excellent. Uttam and Suchitra have given one of their finest performances together. Frought with ego clashes and arguments in their college days, it is greatly comic at times.

Saptapadi is also has the outstanding scene where Krishnendu and Rina Brown enact the death scene from Shakespeare's *Othello*, memorable in its intensity, with both characters realising their love for each other, even as they are struggling to overcome it. Krishnendu and Rina Brown singing '*Ei Poth Jodi Na Shesh Hoy*' astride a bike has been immortalised in public memory as the film's signature song. Scenes where Rina Brown wearing a saree for the first time while Uttam mourns his mother's death, or lovingly packing his bag, or later drunk and in pain, leave a lasting impact on the audience.

Bipasha

Agradoot's *Bipasha* was released in 1962, heralding another milestone in Uttam's and Suchitra's career graphs. *Bipasha* shows the coming together of two very lonely people who have seen life and its struggles without the warmth of loved ones. Bipasha loses her family in the post-Independence clashes, while Diptendu has only his grandmother for family. Things seem fine as the two fall in love and decide to get married. However, fate intervenes and Diptendu leaves his bride-to-be Bipasha and goes missing. Bipasha seeks out her love in Allahabad, where he is frantically searching for his mother, following his maternal uncle's allegations that he is a child out of wedlock!

Though named after the female lead, Bipasha, the film is as much an Uttam show. He, too, excels in scenes where he is the frustrated son, frantically seeking his mother and his identity. In fact, the latter half is about his personal struggle. His body language speaks volumes about a man on the verge of collapse, hardly bothered about romance. A frustrated Diptendu tries to commit suicide, but is rescued by a *swamiji* who turns out to be his father who had deserted the family. In a letter addressed to Diptendu, his father confesses his faults.

Bipasha is a film where Suchitra experimented with herself in more ways than one. Not just her costumes, her mannerisms are varied, too. She dons a short-hair style, then a traditional hairdo. From time to time, she speaks in accented Hindi, given her Bipasha's Punjabi mother's background. Though the latter half of the film is more about Diptendu's turmoil, the steadfast love and belief Bipasha has in Diptendu shine through moments of crisis, too.

The film has it funny moments, too: a boyish Diptendu compliments Bipasha on her looks and makes off in a scooter before she can react! The inclusion of a lengthy, beautifully choreographed dance-drama adds to the culturally rich ambience of the film. *Bipasha* appealed to the aesthetics of both the culturally conscious as well as folk-theatre loving cinegoers. Especially delightful is the first song of the film, where Bipasha celebrates her joy on passing her exams with her friend. As she lip syncs to '*Klanltiro Pothe...*' sung by Sandhya Mukhopadhay, she is simply enthralling!

Kamallata

Director Harisadan Dasgupta's *Kamallata* is a beautiful and poignant tale of a woman who, discouraged by a life full of pain and deceit, becomes a *Baishnabi (a vaishnavite ascetic)*, dedicating her life to Lord Krishna and taking refuge at his feet. *Kamallata* showcases the plight of women, rich or poor, for whom religion becomes a refuge. Filmed in 1969, it is based on the novel *Srikanto* by Sharatchandra Chattopadhyay, set in rural Bengal, and addresses many issues of the times.

Suchitra as Kamallata enacts a variety of emotions: powerful and flexible; principled, yet vulnerable at the same time. Uttam's role as Srikanto, a character based on the life of Sharatchandra Chattopadhyay, is equally interesting in his gradual movement from a non-believer to his acceptance of the universal power that drives everything.

Kamallata explores the dimension of spiritual love where the ultimate faith in the universal force raises two individuals above their worldly needs. Despite their mutual admiration and affection, they are able to go their separate ways, in complete surrender to a higher force.

A scene where Kamal picks flowers for the puja in the morning and Srikanto follows her around while she sings beautifully showcases their growing love for each other. Another memorable and stunningly aesthetic shot shows Srikanto passing a garland for the deity to Kamal. But the action also highlights Srikanto's adoration for Kamal and the desire to bind her to him forever. Such scenes are romantic without a hint of eroticism, taking the film to a different level.

Shot amid the spiralling smoke of incense sticks, Suchitra blends beauty and spirituality in such a way that it is impossible to distinguish one from the other.

Bhajans, such as '*O Mon Kokhon Shuru Kokhon Je Shesh Ke Jane*' sung by Sandhya Mukhopadhay add to the overall ambience of the film. Nirmal Kumar as Gahar Gossain is a summation of religious integrity and magnanimity.

Kamallata, perhaps, presents a new dimension of the Uttam and Suchitra off-screen romance.

Nabarag

Nabarag, made in 1971 by Bijay Bose, was a strong film that dealt with important issues like the relationship between a husband and wife in high society and the upbringing of children in extravagant homes. Narayani is a wide-eyed simple village girl who comes to Kolkata. Here she meets a rich businessman Bipul, who is fascinated by her naïveté, yet ironically seeks to change her once they are married. The change from Narayani to Rina is painful and Suchitra does adequate justice to the role. Rina's inner turmoil at not being able to accept her own son's haughty tantrums is remarkable. Unable to share her pain with her husband, she secretly requests Nanda da, a relative from her village who runs a reform school, to handle her wayward son. Bipul, the distraught father, spends days and nights in search of his son, finally to find him. When realisation dawns on the indulgent father, the family is on their path to happiness once more.

Nabarag is an apt portrayal of high-society life, callous family values and dwindling morals. It also shows Suchitra in a way she is rarely presented: in bits and pieces of skin show, shots in a swimsuit and even scenes under the shower. However, this does not seem out of place in the film. The song '*Ami Jene Shune Beesh Korechi Paan*' is beautifully picturised on Suchitra and depicts Rina's misery at her changed lifestyle and her difficulty in coming to terms with it. The film has suspense, especially when Raja, their son, goes missing.

Har Mana Har

Released in 1972, *Har Mana Har*, directed by Salil Sen was based on the story of Tarashankar Bandhopadhay. The film is a family entertainer with many songs, classic romantic scenes and some tragic moments. A later film of Uttam and Suchitra, *Har Mana Har* drew out mature performances from both, and the chemistry between them is refined and muted.

Binu is an artist who also runs an orphanage. He meets Nira in a friend's house. Nira, who has fled from home to avoid a marriage she was being coerced into by her cousins, accepts the job of a teacher in Binu's orphanage. Once there, Nira tries to improve the conditions of the orphanage and give the children the love they crave for. In the process, Binu and Nira are drawn to each other. Amidst nursing a mental patient Protima (who used to take care of the orphanage earlier) and tolerating rumours of being in a relationship with her, Binu is unable to convince Nira that his love for her is genuine. Anger, frustration, and suspicion separate the couple, to unite them, years later when the truth is laid bare to Nira and misconceptions are sorted out.

Har Mana Har is a happy-go-lucky film in the beginning, with a singing Binu playing with the children in the orphanage or Nira basking in the love the children give her. The attraction between Binu and Nira within the confines of the orphanage has been handled in a mature way, befitting their age and position.

Though not overtly romantic, the film has romance running through it in the mutual dependence of the two characters, their common sensibilities and their concern for the children of the orphanage. The scenes where Nira sings '*Ei Akash Notun, Batash Notun Shobi Tomar Jonno*' in the garden within the orphanage like young girl in love, is very romantic.

In a particularly intense moment in the film, Nira seeks Binu's blessings after having cleared her Master's degree. The scene is well shot. Binu wants to give her a portrait of hers but can't. Regretting this, he plucks a flower instead, from a nearby flower vase, and puts it in her hair and says, '*Chobi eke debo bole chhilam, phul diye sajiye dilam*' (I had promised you a picture; I have completed the picture with the flower).

A happy ending and a mature love story make *Har Mana Har* a special film. Uttam's bohemian character and love for art are special features of the film. The film also shows the problems faced by a single working woman. The latter half of the film shows the poignant inner struggle of both Uttam and Suchitra coming to terms with living without each other.

And despite its many flaws, an Uttam and Suchitra starrer shall always remain *Oti Uttam*—a cut above the rest.

7

If Music be the Food of Love

My song will sit in the pupils of your eyes,
And will carry your sight into the heart of things.
And when my voice is silent in death,
My song will speak in your living heart.

Rabindranath Tagore

The origin of Bengali film music can be traced to two stalwarts, Raichand Boral and Pankaj Mullick. Both of them joined the Indian Broadcasting Company, the forerunner of All India Radio (AIR) in 1927. Mullick was a conductor and music organiser for the orchestra at Chitra cinema during the screening of two silent films: *Chashar Meye* (1931) and *Chorkanta* (1931). Boral, the father of Indian film music, introduced playback singing in Indian films. He is credited with fusing the *ghazal* style of singing from North India with 19th-century Bengali songs. He successfully directed music for about 150 films.

Raichand and Mullick made a tremendous team. The duo composed music for the first Bengali talkie *Dena Paona* (1931), produced by New Theatres. They composed music again for a New Theatres production called *Bhagya Chakra* (1935). This was later adapted in

Hindi, by Nitin Bose, and named *Dhoop Chhaon* (1935), a pathbreaking film that introduced playback singing in Indian films for the first time.

With the talent and direction of stalwarts like Kaji Nazrul Islam, experiments with music began in right earnest. The stage seemed set for experimentation and new sounds began to emerge from Bengali films. There were other music directors like Sudhin Dasgupta, Salil Chowdhury, Robin Chatterjee who made their contribution to Bengali film music. Film music gradually acquired a separate identity, and played a crucial role in ensuring a film's popularity.

Between the 1950s and the 1970s, intriguing compositions explored new dimensions in film music. While Western effects were fused with classical music, folk music and several rural tunes were also influenced by contemporary music.

Stalwarts, such as Manna Dey, Manabendra Mukherjee, Dhananjoy Bhattacharya, Akhil Bandhu Ghosh, Satinath Mukherjee brought freshness to film music through their experiments. Though these singers and composers did not always work with classical numbers, they were influenced by classical legends, such as Tarapodo Chakraborty, Viswadev Chatterjee and Gyanendra Prosad Goswami. On the other hand, compositions of Shyamal Mitra, SD Burman, and Nirmalendu Chowdhury had a rustic charm and a romantic flavour.

Bengali film industry greatly benefited from these experiments since music became as inseparable a selling point for a film as the names of the actors and their histrionic abilities.

Film music plays a dual role. On the one hand, it lends poignancy to the emotions portrayed in a scene and carries forward the story. On the other hand, it advertises and popularises the film. Uttam and Suchitra films took full advantage of film music to popularise films even before they were released. Pamphlets of songs would be released before a film and at times, Uttam and Suchitra would endorse these songs so that the audience would flock to the halls to watch the film. Radio programmes often aired these songs, too, before the release of the film.

Before the advent of playback singing, actors would sing their own songs. Given a song's role in making a film popular, singing actors were always preferred. Several actors including Kanan Devi, Pahari Sanyal and Asit Baran were considered singing actors. Kanan Devi's songs often contributed substantially to the success of her films. With the growth of playback singing, these artistes had to choose between either singing or acting. While some became full-fledged singers, others chose acting.

The growing popularity of films attracted more and more musicians and singers to the Bengali film industry. With the tremendous popularity of film songs, most singers and musicians became household names and stars in their own right. Though this resulted in the commercialisation of the music industry, the quality of these productions was always maintained.

While commercialisation of the music industry drew a large number of talented musicians and singers to the industry, it also had undesirable fallouts: it became increasingly formulaic since experimentation with different musical styles and sounds was discouraged. In a commerce-driven industry, if a particular song became a hit, every other music director composed a similar tune.

One name that made a difference to music in Bengal is Kazi Nazrul Islam. He wrote and composed music for songs in a style that was a blend of Hindustani classical music, folk music from India and the Middle East, as well as Western music. The huge volume of songs produced by Kazi Nazrul Islam provided a fillip to the entire film music industry still in the early stages of recording film music and playback singing. Till the 1950s, Nazrul and his contemporary music composers and lyricists dominated popular music. Rabindra Sangeet, a genre of songs by Rabindranath Tagore, which had considerably influenced film music, became popular again in the 1960s. Music in Uttam and Suchitra starrers *Nabarag* and *Shapmochan* were deeply influenced by Rabindra Sangeet.

The emergence of great popular Bengali film music coincided with Uttam's and Suchitra's poularity from the 1950s to the 1970s. Robin Chatterjee, Salil Chowdhury, Himangshu Dutta, Anupam Ghatak and Kamal Dasgupta made a lasting impact on an entire generation and greatly influenced Bengali music trends. Lyricists, such as Salil Chowdhury, Gauri Prasanna Majumdar, Pronob Roy, Sailen Roy, Mukul Datta, Ajoy Bhattacharya, Pulak Bondopadhyay, Nishikanta, Shyamal Gupta and Bhaskar Basu wrote great compositions that mesmerised cinephiles. Bengali film singers made their presence felt in the national music industry and became legends in their own right. Names, such as Shyamal Mitra, Hemanta Kumar, Satinath Mukhopadhay, Akhilbondhu Ghosh, Dhananjoy Bhattacharya, Manabendra Mukhopadhay and Sandhya Mukhopadhay spelt success for film music.

In *Harano Sur*, Roma sings '*Tumi Je Amar*' repeatedly to remind her husband of her existence; the song and the melody are embedded in the storyline itself. In *Saptapadi*, there is interesting fusion of Western and Indian music in the song '*Ebar Kali Tomay Khabo*', where Western music is used to depict the class difference between the lead characters of the song. The composition was like a fresh breath of air that delighted everyone, especially the youth, by its exuberance. The city girl-versus-traditional boy fight is always a good recipe for drawing young crowds. In the same film, '*Ei Path Jodi Na Sesh Hoy*' picturised on Uttam-Suchitra on a bike became the epitome of youthful romance for an entire generation. In *Agnipariksha*, when Tapasi sings '*Jodi Bhul Kore, Bhul Madhur Holo*' in the voice of Sandhya Mukhopadhyay, she expresses her happiness at Kiriti accidentally touching her hands, something that she could not express in words. In *Kamallata*, when Gahar Gossain sings '*Kokhon Suru Kokhon Je Sesh*', he seems to be expressing Kamallata and Srikanto's feelings of piety at multiple levels. The song describes a spiritual romance portrayed in the film. '*Nir Chhoto Khoti Nei*', picturised on Uttam and Suchitra in *Indrani* shows a married couple in love. Again in *Sagarika*, when Arun pours his heart out in the song '*Amar Sopne Dekha Raj Konna Thake*', many young men sing along.

The 1950s and 1960s marked the golden age of Bengali cinema. Much credit for that goes to the music composers and singers, in addition to the Uttam and Suchitra pairing.

As film music gained in popularity, singers like Hemanta Kumar, Shyamal Mitra, Sandhya Mukhopadhay and Geeta Dutt also acquired unprecedented fame. Such was the abundance of talent in Bengal in these two decades that its film industry was totally self-sufficient in terms of music composers, especially singers, and there was no need to turn to popular Bollywood singers. Hemanta Kumar, Sandhya Mukhopadhay and Geeta Dutt lent their voices to many songs picturised on Uttam-Suchitra. It is difficult to imagine a romantic Uttam and Suchitra starrer without the voice of these singers.

Lyricist Gauri Prasanna Majumdar once said that had it not been for Hemanta Kumar and Sandhya Mukhopadhay, neither the Uttam and Suchitra films nor the songs would have been as popular.

Hemanta Kumar worked as a composer, too, for films like *Shapmochon* and *Harano Sur*. His voice came to be so identified with Uttam that one without the other seemed incomplete. Despite their age difference, the two were great friends. Uttam would have many musical sessions with Hemanta Kumar in his house, where both would sing. Hemanta Kumar once said, 'Thank God, Uttam is only an actor and not a singer. Otherwise he would have deprived many singers of their livelihood.'

The producer of *Mantra Mugdha* (1977) had once wanted to rope in Uttam as the hero of his film. On hearing the script, Uttam refused, saying the role would suit the younger actor Soumitra Chatterjee. A disappointed producer approached Hemanta Kumar. Immediately the singer visited Uttam to enquire about what happened. When Uttam explained his problem, Hemanta Kumar said, 'While I understand your problem, no one but you can do justice to my songs and how can I sing for someone else?' Incidentally, Uttam did not play this part; eventually it went to Soumitra Chatterjee. Songs sung by Hemanta Kumar for Uttam in his films became huge hits. Starting with *Shapmochon,* an Uttam and Suchitra film, their combination became as popular as the Raj Kapoor-Mukesh combination in Bollywood.

Uttam and Suchita scorched the Bengali screen from 1950 to 1970 with not only their screen presence but also their acting prowess. The unbeatable pair acted in some 30 films over two decades, most of which were runaway box-office hits.

Sare Chuattor (1953), the first film of Uttam and Suchitra, ushered in the most glorious period of Bengali cinema. In the 1950s, the youth craved for something new which the young and good-looking couple seemed to offer.

Uttam and Suchitra infused Bengali cinema with a certain glamour and stardom hitherto lacking. Not only did they revive the audience's interest in Bengali cinema, but also lent magic to it.

A poster of *Ekti Raat* (1956), directed by Chitta Basu. *Ekti Raat*'s melodrama and underlying sensuality was a clever theme, happily lapped up the audience.

A scene from *Ekti Raat*, a rather bold film for its times. Two people are happily married to their respective spouses when a turn of rather hilarious events brings them together at night in the same room.

Uttam-Suchitra starrers often traded the backdrop of rural rusticity for that of a slick city, depicting a lifestyle not shown earlier.

What added to the romantic pairing were the excellent sets, the soft nuances of black-and-white films, haunting music and a dreamy ambience.

Be it gazing at each other forlornly or other romantic intimacies, romance as portrayed by Uttam and Suchitra has not been paralled in Bengali cinema.

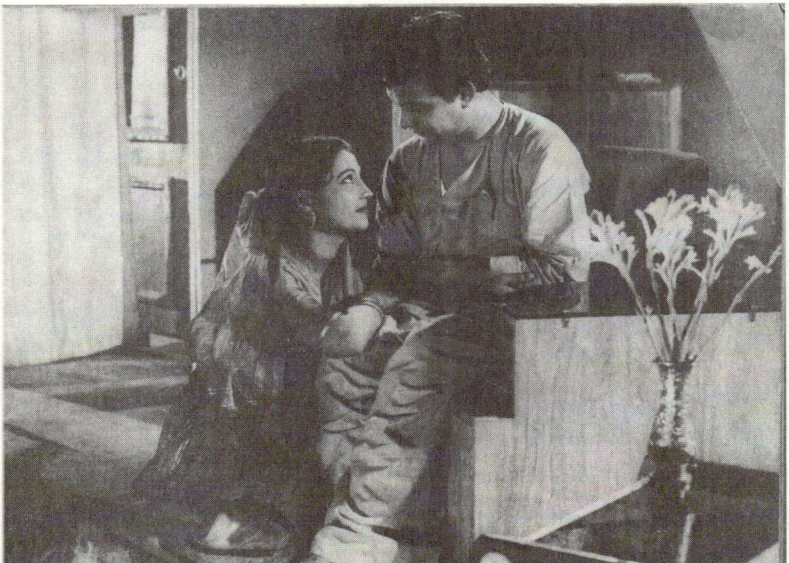

Despite their glamour, Uttam and Suchitra essayed traditional and subtly sensuous roles to perfection.

With *Agnipariksha* (1954) a hitherto conservative Bengali cinema showed scenes of physical intimacy on screen for the first time. Soon a well-orchestrated climactic dénouement, where the hero and heroine could be seen rushing into each other's arms after several misunderstandings and ordeals, became the most successful romantic formula.

In the words of Madhabi Mukherjee, a famous contemporary actress, Uttam and Suchitra were like 'Radha and Krishna on the silver screen'.

Uttam and Suchitra's celluloid escapades covered the entire repertoire from the melodramatic and sublime to the inordinately mellow.

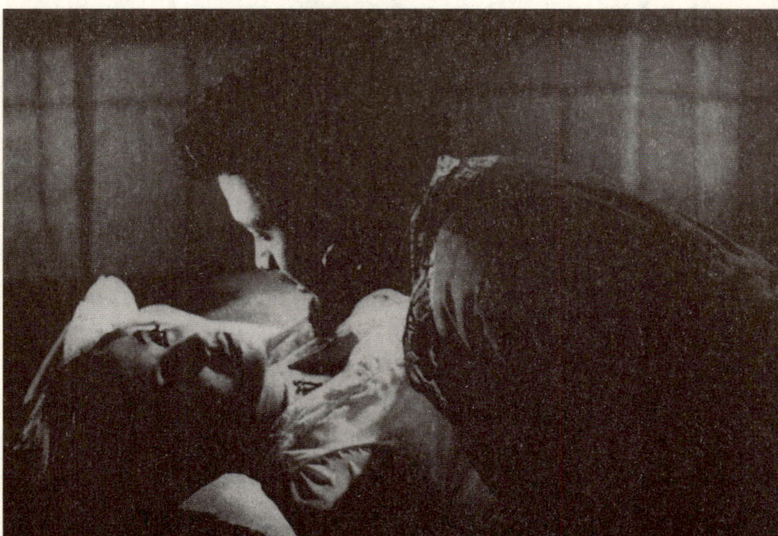

Drama, passion and pathos abounded in a typical Uttam-Suchitra starrer.

Some stories transcended the boundaries of ordinary story-telling into something more sublime through the sheer interpretation of this talented duo.

Harano Sur (1957) directed by Ajoy Kar combined the beauty of the countryside and the glamour of the city to highlight the poignant central theme of recovery from memory loss.

Chandranth (1957) directed by Kartik Chatterjee was a moving tale. Set in Varanasi, India, the film shows Uttam and Suchitra in intense roles, their chemistry playing out beautifully even under tragic circumstances.

A poster of *Indrani* (1958) directed by Niren Lahiri, a blockbuster of the times.

A poster of *Bipasha* (1962) directed by Agradoot marked another milestone in the duo's careers.

In *Bipasha*, a story by Tarashankar Bandopadhyay, the young, energetic couple exuded the same undying appeal as they would decades later.

Kamallata (1969), a Saratchandra Chatterjee masterpiece, portrayed Uttam and Suchitra in muted and mellow performances, contrary to their glamorous and stunning personalities.

Nabarag (1971) directed by Bijoy Bose portrayed high-society life, callous family values and dwindling morals, driving home a strong message on how children ought to be brought up.

Nabarag, a story by Ashutosh Mukherjee saw some sterling performances from a more mature Uttam and Suchitra.

Har Mana Har (1972) directed by Salil Sen based on a story by Tarashankar Bandopadhayay, was a complete family entertainer with many songs, classic romantic scenes and some tragic moments.

Raj Kapoor and Nargis Dutt worked together in 16 films from 1948 to 1956, including six of Raj Kapoor's own productions. Their undeniable on-screen chemistry was a reflection of their love for each other.

Dev Anand and Suraiya co-starred in six films between 1948 and 1951 and became a very popular pair. Suraiya was prevented from marrying Dev Anand because they came from different religious backgrounds.

Since their first film in 1951, Dilip Kumar and Madhubala hit it off onscreen as well as offscreen and gave some of the finest classics of Hindi cinema. Their stormy relationship, which lasted about eight years, wove magic into their films. Madhubala died in 1969 at the age of 36.

A talented actress, Waheeda Rehman was spotted by noted actor and director, Guru Dutt, with whom she worked from 1957 to 1962 in five of his classics. When their off-screen chemistry came under scrutiny, they drifted apart both personally and professionally. Guru Dutt, who was already married, died soon after, in 1964.

Rajesh Khanna and Sharmila Tagore teamed up professionally to form one of the most sensuous and passionate couples in Indian cinema. They sizzled onscreen even though in real life they did not share the same personal bond.

Dharmendra and Hema Malini were one of the best-looking couples of their times. Dharmendra was already married when he met Hema Malini but the two, with their amazing chemistry, did eventually marry each other.

In *Harano Sur,* at a certain stage when Uttam wasn't available to dub, Hemanta Kumar was roped in to fill in for the hero. In many films starring Uttam and Suchitra, Hemanta Kumar made an impact as the romantic voice of Uttam that wooed Suchitra. '*Suno Bandhu Suno*' and '*Jhor Utteche*' became popular with viewers. Other popular Uttam-Hemanta Kumar songs include '*Nir Chhoto Khoti Nei*' from *Indrani* and '*Ei Poth Jodi Na Shesh Hoy*' from *Saptapadi.* And when '*Ei Betha Ki Je Betha Bojhe Na Anjane*' from *Dhanni Meye* (1971), sung by Hemanta Kumar, became extremely popular, Uttam is said to have regretted that it was not picturised on him.

Similarly, Geeta Dutt and Sandhya Mukhopadhay lent their voices to the beautiful songs picturised on Suchitra in many films where she starred with Uttam. People still remember Sandhya Mukhopadhay's rendition of '*Gane More*' in *Agnipariksha,* just as they remember Geeta Dutt's voice in '*Tumi Je Amar*' from *Harano Sur* and '*Nir Chhoto Khoti Nei*' from *Indrani.* The mood that these songs created was one of pure ecstasy.

'*Tumi Je Amar*' was adapted for a Hindi version '*Chale Hum Kahaan*' in *Police* (1958) in the voices of Hemanta Kumar and Geeta Dutt, but the Hindi adaptation was not as successful.

Suchitra, who was interested in singing herself, is said to have taken special interest in the picturisation of many important songs. She understood that the efforts of the singer would be wasted if her lip sync and picturisation were not right. In *Indrani* as she goes '*Jhonok Jhonok Konok Kankon Baaje*', she transports us to a different world. Her smile, the arch of her eyebrows and other expressions are as much a part of the beauty of the song as the lyrics themselves. In the sensually beautiful '*Tumi Je Amar*', one can't help but smile along with her, delighted by the passion in her facial expression.

Suchitra shared a rare rapport with Geeta Dutt. She sang all the songs for Suchitra in *Indrani*. Popular numbers, such as '*Jhonok Jhonok Konok Kankon Baaje*', '*Nir Chhoto Khoti Nei*' and '*Ogo Sundoro*' are fondly remembered even today. However, Geeta Dutt sang for Suchitra only in Bengali films.

Sandhya Mukhopadhay also sang many of the hit songs picturised on Suchitra in many Uttam and Suchitra films. The two shared a personal relationship, too. In films, such as *Bipasha, Sagarika, Pothe Holo Deri* and *Smriti Tuku Thak* (1960), Sandhya Mukhopadhay sang for Suchitra. Songs, such as '*E Shudhu Ganer Din*', '*Tumi Na Hoy Rohite Kache*', '*Ami Sapne Tomay Dekhechi*' and '*Monero Madhuri Mishaye*' were often an embodiment of the popular melodramatic films of that era.

Coincidentally, both ladies shunned publicity and fame once they retired from public life. While Suchitra took the extreme step of secluding herself, Sandhya Mukhopadhay refrained from taking on too much work. It is indeed difficult to distinguish the magic of these singers from the magic of actors for whom they sang.

Songs featured in Uttam and Suchitra films celebrated the idyllic on-screen romance of the star pair. These songs were expressions of lovers' sentiments, pent up frustrations, happy and poignant moments that were part of the roller-coaster ride that the duo experienced in their films. Gauri Prasanna Majumdar wrote the most soulful lyrics for Uttam and Suchitra films. Always identifiable with the duo, he was their preferred lyricist. Many a times, they would recommend him to a producer. Majumdar said in an interview that while writing lyrics for Uttam and Suchitra films, he would not only keep in mind what the scene demanded but also how the duo would look singing the lyrics. He says his song '*Gane More*' in *Agniparikska* was the turning point in his career.

Much of the credit for popularising the Uttam and Suchitra songs also goes to the radio, which helped in marketing their films. Radio programmes like *Anurodher Ashor*, a programme of requests, made viewers tune in and listen to their favourite songs from these films.

Among the many composers, Robin Chatterjee was responsible for influencing the taste of film-music lovers with his occasional modern touch. His compositions for Uttam and Suchitra films did much to popularise their films. '*Ghum Ghum Chand*' picturised on Suchitra in the *Sobar Upore* (1955), sung by Sandhya Mukhopadhay, became a super hit. The Vaisnavik bhajan '*O Mon Kokhon Shuru Kokhon Je Shesh Ke Jane*' that he composed for *Kamallata* also became very popular.

Robin Chatterjee was a versatile composer with a wide repertoire, and composed according to the requirements of the film. In *Sagarika*, his composition '*Amar Sapne Dekha Rajkonya*' became a big hit. He made good use of Salil Chowdhury and Sudhin Dasgupta and revolutionised film tunes with his fine use of the piano in several of his compositions.

Robin Chatterjee's compositions in some major Uttam and Suchitra starrers, such as *Sagarika, Shilpi, Bipasha, Pothe Holo Deri, Chandranath* (1957) and *Kamallata*, which were a rage with the masses, are perennial favourites. And undoubtedly, his compositions added to the romantic fervour of the star pair.

In a way, the relationship between Uttam and Suchitra films and the music in them was symbiotic. One without the other would have been unimaginable.

Actor June Maliah says in an interview, 'I think the entire Uttam package was unbeatable. Not only were the films he acted in, superb; he was part of the winning Uttam and Suchitra combination and all the films had mind-blowing songs with beautiful lyrics.'

Suchitra's combination with both Geeta Dutta and Sandhya Mukhopadhay was appreciated as much as Uttam's permanent bond with Hemanta Kumar.

During the recording of *'Ei Path Jodi Na Sesh Hoy'* in *Saptapadi,* the filmmakers thought that the song was easy to sing, and they need not involve famous singer Sandhya Mukhopadhay. So another well-known singer was roped in. Yet despite several takes, she could not do justice to the song, especially to the part where Suchitra needed to hum *'la la la la'*. The chosen singer was promptly replaced and Sandhya Mukhopadhay brought in to sing the song, which then went on to become very popular.

Whether the Uttam and Suchitra pairing would have been as successful, had it not been for their films' music and songs, is a matter of debate, but music and songs remained an integral part of Uttam's and Suchitra's image in the hearts of people.

With the departure of Suchitra from films and the untimely demise of Uttam, Bangla *adhunik* (popular) music suffered a severe blow. The biggest challenge would be to find the right inspiration to make good music once again.

Some songs that added to the magic of the Uttam and Suchitra pairing:

Song: *'Tumi Je Amar'*
Film: *Harano Sur*
Singer: Geeta Dutt

Song: *'Ei Poth Jodi Na Shesh Hoy'*
Film: *Saptapadi*
Singers: Hemanta Kumar Mukhopadhay, Sandhya Mukhopadhay

Song: *'Surjo Dobar Pala'*
Film: *Indrani*
Singer: Hemanta Kumar Mukhopadhay

Song: *'Gaane More'*
Film: *Agnipariksha*
Singer: Sandhya Mukhopadhay

Song: *'Jhonok Jhonok'*
Film: *Indrani*
Singer: Geeta Dutt

Song: *'Ami Jene Shune Bish Korechhi Paan'*
Film: *Nabarag*
Singer: Sandhya Mukhopadhay

Song: *'Jodi Bhul Kore'*
Film: *Agnipariksha*
Singer: Sandhya Mukhopadhay

Song: *'Ogo Sundoro'*
Film: *Indrani*
Singers: Geeta Dutt

Song: *'Nir Chhoto'*
Film: *Indrani*
Singers: Hemanta Kumar Mukhopadhay, Geeta Dutt

Song: *'Ebar Kaali Tomay Khaabo'*
Film: *Saptapadi*
Singer: Hemanta Kumar Mukhopadhay

Song: *'Sono Bondhu Sono'*
Film: *Shapmochan*
Singer: Hemanta Kumar Mukhopadhay

Song: *'Amar Sopne Dekha Rajkonna Thake'*
Film: *Sagarika*
Singer: Shyamal Mitra

Song: *'Aaj Dujonar'*
Film: *Harano Sur*
Singers: Hemanta Kumar Mukhopadhay

Song: *'Gum Gum Chand'*
Film: *Sabar Uporey*
Singer: Sandhya Mukhopadhay

Song: *'O Bashi Baje'*
Movie: *Ekti Raat*
Singer: Sandhya Mukhopadhay

Song: *'Nupurer Gunjane'*
Film: *Shilpi*
Singer: Geeta Dutta

Song: *'Ke Tumi Amare Dako'*
Film: *Agnipariksha*
Singer: Sandhya Mukhopadhay

8

Bollywood Bound

The traveller has to knock at every alien door to come to his own,
And one has to wander through all the outer worlds,
To reach the innermost shrine at the end.

Rabindranath Tagore

Satyajit Ray and Mrinal Sen, two of Bengal's finest filmmakers, tried their hand at making Hindi films. Most parallel Hindi films of their times had a Bengali sub-context involving Hindi film actors, such as Shabana Azmi, Smita Patil, Naseeruddin Shah and Om Puri. In recent times, many Bengali directors have used not only Hindi film actors, but also professionals from the Hindi film industry for camera work, stylisation, etc. Actors, such as Amitabh Bachchan, Preity Zinta, Aishwarya Rai and Ajay Devgn have been associated with Bengali production houses, and take pride in having worked in Bengali cinema.

There was an era in the history of national cinema when everything in Bengali cinema was equated with good cinema. Between 1950 and 1970, Bengali cinema boasted of the best technicians, good scripts and great actors, and Hindi cinema embraced some of this talent. Stalwarts of Bengali cinema, such as PC Barua, Kanan Devi, Bimal Roy and Hemanta Kumar began their creative journey in Bengali cinema, even as they went on to make their mark in Bollywood. Bengal had always been inclined towards literature, and boasted of great writers like Rabindranath Tagore, Bankim Chandra Chattopadhyay and Sharat Chandra Chattopadhyay. Such was the respect and adulation that filmstars from Bengal commanded that many Hindi filmmakers invited them to grace the Bollywood screen. Kanan Devi was one such example. Apart from being Bengal's first film actress, she was much in demand in Hindi films, too. Raj Kapoor, who worked with Chhobi Biswas, once said that he had yet to see talent like Chhobi Biswas on Indian screen. Most Hindi film actors would consider it a privilege to be invited to work in Bengali films.

Uttam and Suchitra, who worked in the Bengali film industry for almost three decades, also tested the waters in Hindi cinema. Whether it was destiny or wrong timing, both the stars, though hugely popular in Bengal, were only marginally successful in Hindi films.

The Hindi film industry gained prominence because it appealed to a national audience. Working in Hindi cinema guaranteed a wider audience and the scope for working in bigger-budget films. Talented actors, directors, musicians, technicians and cameramen moved from Bengal to Hindi cinema. Jaya Bhadhuri, Rakhee, Sharmila Tagore, Tanuja, Moushumi Chatterjee, Ashok Kumar, Utpal Dutt, Pradeep Kumar, Biswajit, Keshto Mukherjee, Joy Mukherjee and Mithun Chakraborty were some of the actors who shifted to Hindi cinema. Directors, such as Satyajit Ray, Mrinal Sen, Bimal Roy,

Asit Sen, Hrishikesh Mukherjee and Ritwik Ghatak contributed enormously to Indian and Bengali cinema.

Hemanta Kumar, Kishore Kumar, Manna Dey, Salil Chowdhury, SD Burman, RD Burman, to name a few, added quality compositions to Hindi film music. While Bengali films always had strong scripts mostly based on literature, Hindi cinema followed suit. Thus glamour was ably complemented by a strong story. Many Bengali films were adapted into Hindi, and many Hindi films were inspired by Bengali films. Hindi filmmakers would either rope in fresh faces for an adaptation, or use actors who had acted in the original Bengali film, provided they appealed to a Hindi film audience. That Bengali films artfully combined a realistic style of storytelling with the ingredients for popular entertainment was an advantage while adapting Bengali films into Hindi.

Some Bengali filmmakers adapted their films into Hindi to gain a wider audience. Asit Sen adapted three of his hit Bengali films into Hindi. He remade *Uttar Falguni* as *Mamta* in Hindi, with Suchitra in the dual role of a prostitute and her daughter; *Dweep Jweley Jay*, a Bengali hit, into *Khamoshi* (1969) with Rajesh Khanna and Waheeda Rehman in the lead. This was followed by *Safar*, a remake of *Chalachal* (1956), another of his Bengali hits. Ajoy Kar's *Saat Pake Bandha* was remade into *Kora Kagaz* (1974) in Hindi by Anil Ganguly, with Jaya Bhadhuri and Vijay Anand in the lead roles.

With Hindi cinema's rising popularity and mass appeal, actors from Bengali cinema tried to woo Hindi audience, too, especially after they had made a name for themselves on home turf.

Some Hindi films had an unmistakable Bengali cultural flavour. The Bengali film *Kabuliwala* (1961) was remade in Hindi by Bimal Roy, with Balraj Sahni. Though not as successful as the original Bengali version, *Kabuliwala* was appreciated by the Hindi film audience. Similarly, Roy's *Do Bigha Zameen* (1953), starring Balraj Sahni and Nirupa Roy, was an iconic film in its times and remains a classic even today.

Bengali novelists, such as Sharat Chandra Chattopadhyay and Bankim Chandra Chattopadhyay were popular with the masses for their understanding and depiction of social and economic issues. Films based on Sharat Chandra's stories appealed to Hindi filmmakers. Remakes of his *Devdas*, for example, have had a tremendous impact on cinegoers. Cinematically adapted by Bimal Roy in 1955, the film earned Dilip Kumar the title of Tragedy King, as well as great popularity. Sharat Chandra's *Parineeta* was picturised by Bimal Roy in 1953 with Meena Kumari in the lead role. The remakes of *Devdas* (2002) and *Parineeta* (2005) by Sanjay Leela Bansali and Pradeep Sarkar respectively were highly successful.

Bimal Roy's landmark Hindi film *Bandini* (1963), on people involved in crimes, was based on the work of Bengali writer Jorasandho. *Nishipadma* (1970) was later adapted as *Amar Prem* (1972). Another Bollywood classic *Nagin* (1954), based on the story of Bengali writer Tarashankar Bandhopadhay and scripted by the great dramatist Bijon Bhattacharya, was extremely popular, with long runs in theatres even outside India. Incidentally, the music of *Nagin* scored by Hemanta Kumar, was a huge hit, too. Legend has it that a theatre in Lahore had to be re-christened 'Nagin' because of the number of shows it held of the film.

Kolkata and Bengal have featured repeatedly in Hindi films. Producer-director Himanshu Ray, of

Mumbai Talkies fame, his actress wife Devika Rani and scriptwriter Niranjan Pal had arrived in Bollywood during the silent movie era. The Bengali presence in Bollywood was strongly represented by Sasadhar Mukherjee, Subodh Mukherjee and Prabodh Mukherjee, Bimal Roy and his team, and in many ways by the great Guru Dutt, who was born and brought up partly in Kolkata. Guru Dutt was deeply influenced by Bengali culture. His films like *Pyaasa* (1957) and *Sahib Bibi Aur Ghulam* (1962) were set in Kolkata.

At the height of their popularity Uttam and Suchitra explored the world of Hindi films. Well-known names in Bengali cinema, both were relatively new to a national audience. In hindsight, the limited success of this golden couple in Hindi cinema may be due to the fact that they were never cast in a Hindi film as a romantic couple. Had this happened, perhaps, Uttam and Suchitra would have worked their magic in Hindi cinema, too.

Suchitra did seven films in Hindi—*Devdas* (1955), *Musafir* (1957), *Champakali* (1957), *Bambai Ka Babu* (1960), *Sarhad* (1960), *Mamta*, and *Aandhi*. Except in Gulzar's *Aandhi* (1972), Suchitra's presence was somewhat mediocre in Hindi films, perhaps because of the unfamiliar language and territory.

When Suchitra made her debut in Hindi films in 1953 as Paro in *Devdas*, she was already an established actor in Bengal. She agreed to do the role (initially offered to Meena Kumari) for two reasons—the opportunity to work with Bimal Roy and the chance to playing a character from Sharat Chandra's famous novel, something she had always desired. Suchitra went on to do many more roles in Bengali films based on characters etched by Sharat Chandra, but this was her first.

Accompanied by her husband, Suchitra went to Mumbai for the shooting of *Devdas* with her friend Dhiren Deb. Suchitra delivered a fine performance in the film. *Devdas*, the story of two childhood friends-turned-lovers pining for each other throughout their lives, was immortalised by a strong cast and diligent direction. Suchitra's simple and measured dialogue delivery added to the pathos of an already sensitive story. *Devdas* fetched Suchitra both critical acclaim and popularity.

Dhiren Deb recalls many interesting anecdotes during this visit. True to her reputation, Suchitra was reserved on the sets. She was noticed by Dilip Kumar, a famous star at that time. He tried to strike up a friendship with Mrs Sen, but she remained aloof. The new face in the Mumbai film industry attracted curious onlookers who had heard much about Suchitra's beauty. Dhiren Deb noted some professional rivalry with Vyjayanthimala, who resented the attention Suchitra received during the shoot from the press and from Dilip Kumar. Being a professional, Suchitra kept to herself and her family once the shoot was over.

Suchitra was nominated for the Filmfare awards for 'Best Actress' category and Vyjayanthimala, was nominated for 'Best Supporting Actress', though the latter insisted that she was the lead actress of the film, and not a supporting actress.

Soon after *Devdas*, Suchitra starred in *Musafir*, a directorial venture by Bimal Roy's editor, Hrishikesh Mukherjee. Suchitra was among the few actors, along with Dilip Kumar, who realised the artistic potential of Hrishikesh Mukherjee. She also had a good rapport with him. When he told her of his desire to make his own film, she expressed a wish to be a part of it. A surprised

Hrishikesh said he could not afford such a highly-paid star. Suchitra is said to have agreed to work in his film for a token amount, to encourage him.

Musafir was the story of a home which saw a frequent change of tenants. The cast included some big names like Dilip Kumar. Suchitra was one of the first tenants (a runaway couple). The film had several stories within a single story, and proved to be far ahead of its times. Predictably, it was not a commercial success and did assure Suchitra a better position in Hindi films. The same year, Suchitra was offered another Hindi film *Champakali* directed by Nandlal Jaswantlal, with big names like Bharat Bhushan and Shubha Khote. The film turned out to be mediocre, bombed at the box office and sank without a trace.

Suchitra returned to Hindi films in 1960, after a break of three years, during which time she worked only in Bengali films. She was approached for two films, both opposite Dev Anand: *Bombai Ka Babu* by Raj Khosla and *Sarhad* with Shankar Mukherjee as director. Both films did moderate business despite Dev Anand's popularity, Suchitra's fine performances, and bold storylines. Dev Anand, who shared a good rapport with her during those days, remembered her as an actor who was immensely beautiful, talented, reserved and professional. He also remembered her lack of camera consciousness during close shots. Not a trained dancer, she put in a lot of effort into her footwork. Said Dev Anand of Suchitra, 'I still remember the sequence where I am casually lying down in a field and ask her to pluck flowers. In that particular shot, my love for her is shown for the first time, despite no physical contact between us except the one occasion when I put a flower in her hair. Suchitra says her dialogue in astonishment, *"Kunwari ladkiyan balon mein phool nahin lagate*" (Unmarried girls do not wear flowers in their hair). No other actor could have performed that romantic scene the way Suchitra did. Again at the climax, during the song "*Chal re sajni*", her eyes spoke more than a hundred dialogues.'

He also remembered Suchitra as an actor who could adapt herself to any character, adding that she had a majestic screen presence, a haunting smile and ample histrionic abilities.

Suchitra had to work twice as hard on her Hindi because of her Bengali accent. The warmth and rapport shared by the two actors was evident in their chemistry. 'She was punctual and would leave the sets as soon as her work was complete. She never wasted time gossiping and talking unnecessarily. She maintained her distance. But she was an excellent human being and respected all. I shared a warm rapport with her and had no ego problems,' said Dev Anand.

Bombai Ka Babu was a daring and bold adventure by Raj Khosla about incestuous romance, a theme that the film deals with sensitively, without actually talking about it. Khosla boldly plays around the topic of brother-sister romance. The camera is often seen panning on Suchitra's form and captures quite openly Dev Anand's open expression of physical love for his on-screen sister. Suchitra is marvellous, especially in the scenes where she is angry and astonished at her brother's odd behaviour. Her conflicting emotions make the character more human.

'At first, I had my reservations about Suchitra, as she was not fluent in Hindi. Raj Khosla asked me to be patient and watch the results while performing. I was proven very wrong. And though not a trained dancer, she was superb in the song sequence, *"Dekhne Mein Bhola Hai"*,' admitted Dev Anand.

If rumours are to be believed, during the shooting of *Bombai Ka Babu* in Kulu, the producer of the film was attracted to Suchitra and made unwarranted advances. Suchitra is supposed to have slapped him in the presence of the unit and threatened to stop work altogether. The wise producer made amends by profusely apologising to her and salvaged his film.

Though Suchitra was appreciated for her totally candid and sensitive performance in *Bombai Ka Babu*, the film did not do as well as expected. Perhaps, the audience could not relate to such a plot or storyline. Suchitra's second film opposite Dev Anand, *Sarhad*, was a total flop and was forgotten soon after its release. Dev Anand confessed that *Sarhad* didn't do much for either actor, except recognising them as a good pair.

Suchitra tasted success in Bollywood in Asit Sen's *Mamta.* With illustrious co-stars like Ashok Kumar and Dharmendra, Suchitra delivered one of the finest performances of her career, in the double role a mother and daughter—the prostitute who toils to give her daughter a respectable life, and the daughter who unknowingly defends her mother in a murder trial. In fact, the mother had committed the murder to save her daughter.

The last Hindi film Suchitra acted in was her biggest hit, *Aandhi.* Made by Gulzar, *Aandhi* is the story of woman politician, Aarti Devi, played by Suchitra. The film saw Suchitra playing the role of a woman much older than herself. Her captivating character exudes strength and authority. During a work visit, she stays in a hotel where her former husband is a manager. The story unfolds in a series of alternate flashbacks, showing their initial romance and marriage, and their being drawn to each other again culminating in a political backlash for Aarti Devi. Disillusioned by dirty party politics she decides to give up her career but this time around her husband reminds her of her duty to the people.

The film became highly controversial as it supposedly bore close resemblance to the life of Indira Gandhi. It was banned for two months, which attracted even more attention to the film. And Suchitra's performance was highly appreciated by the audience.

Industry gossip has it that during the making of *Aandhi,* Sanjeev Kumar was smitten by Suchitra. After *Aandhi,* both actors became friends and Sanjeev Kumar even attended Moon Moon's wedding. *Aandhi* gave Suchitra the kind of adulation and respect that she had always desired as an actor. Gulzar, who shares a special relationship with Suchitra, says that he was aware of Suchitra's strong persona and he conceived the role especially for her. Suchitra wanted to dub for *Aandhi* in her own voice—a wish to prove her Hindi diction. Though her Hindi diction in the film had scope for much improvement, *Aandhi* finally established Suchitra as a successful actor in Hindi cinema.

It might be noted that working in Hindi films was not necessary for an actress of Suchitra's calibre. Yet being a national actress did add to her glamour quotient back home, though she gradually faded out from films a year or two later.

Uttam began his career in films in 1947, incidentally, with the role of an extra in a Hindi film named *Mayador.*

Uttam was at this point struggling to get a toehold in films after being successful in Bengali theatre. Contrary to his expectations of a great beginning, *Mayador* was never released. Taking it as a warning about his future in Hindi films, he returned home to try his luck in Bengali cinema, where he achieved phenomenal success after the initial hiccups. Uttam did not work in Hindi films until much later, when he was a matinee idol in Bengali cinema. In fact, many of his admirers, including those in Bollywood, had believed that had Uttam continued to work in Hindi films from an early stage in his career, rather than later he would have posed tough competition to some of the biggest Bollywood heroes of those times. An untiring learner, he knew he would have to improve his diction if he were to make it as a national actor. He took classes in spoken Hindi and Urdu to polish his diction. However, when he realised that his intrinsic Bengali mannerisms and style appealed more to a Bengali than a Hindi audience, so he decided to concentrate on Bengali films.

As Uttam's admirers will corroborate, it was his nature to go after something that he had not achieved. It was, perhaps, this quality that drove him to try his luck in Hindi films again. However, he starred as a hero in just a handful of films over a decade: *Chhoti Si Mulaqat*, *Amanush* (1975), *Anand Ashram* (1977) and *Dooriyan* (1979). Interestingly, in spite of the limited number of Hindi films that Uttam worked in, he lip sync-ed for songs by the finest Bollywood playback singers including Hemant Kumar, Mohammad Rafi, Kishore Kumar, Shyamal Mitra and Manna Dey.

Anand is said to have been inspired by the friendship between Raj Kapoor and Hrishikesh Mukherjee. Uttam and Shashi Kapoor were the original choices, though finally Rajesh Khanna and Amitabh Bachchan were cast in the lead roles.

Sharmila Tagore, who worked with Uttam in several films, such as *Amanush, Anand Ashram, Dooriyan* and *Amar Prem* (1972) was in awe of the actor. She considered him one of the greatest actors of his time. Negating any comparison with Dilip Kumar, she says, 'Dilip Kumar is a fantastic actor; Uttam was even better. Also, Uttam had much better looks.' Sharmila further adds, 'He remained the top-draw as a romantic hero till his death. He never allowed himself to gain weight and that could be one reason why he retained his romantic appeal to the end. No actor in Mumbai could have that kind of romantic appeal after 30 years in the industry.'

Apart from acting and producing films, Uttam had an indirect influence on Bollywood. Given his unbeatable success record in Bengali films—he acted in over 200 films, most of them hits—Hindi filmmakers were inspired to remake some of his Bengali films in Hindi. While some of these films went on to become hits, many rued the fact that the Uttam touch was missing.

One highly successful, landmark film adapted in Hindi was Nirmal Dey's *Basu Parivar,* which had given Uttam his first taste of success in Bengali cinema. The film was adapted in Hindi by Ram Mukherjee, as *Hum Hindustani* (1960). Uttam's Bengali film *Jeebon Mrityu* by Hiren Nag was remade in Hindi with the same name by Satyen Basu in 1970, with Dharmendra in the lead. Another Bengali film of Uttam's whose remake in Hindi was highly successful was *Sahib, Bibi Aur Ghulam.* The original film of the same name made in 1955 in which Uttam had played the role of Bhootnath, was very successful. The success of the Hindi version of the film is attributed to Guru Dutt's understanding of Bengali culture and the aristocracy in Kolkata. *Sahib, Bibi Aur Ghulam* made an enormous impact on both the Bengali and Hindi audience, especially in its depiction of the British Raj in Kolkata.

Bhranti Bilash, a comedy by Uttam, was remade in Hindi as *Angoor* (1982) by Gulzar. The film, starring Sanjeev Kumar and Moushumi Chatterjee, was an adaptation of the Sabitri Chatterjee-Uttam starrer in Bengali. Many claim that Sanjeev Kumar could not match Uttam's performance in the original Bengali film. *Nishipadma*, another Bengali hit featuring Uttam and Sabitri Chatterjee, was remade in Hindi as *Amar Prem* by Shakti Samanta. The film won much critical acclaim, with both Rajesh Khanna and Sharmila Tagore giving brilliant performances.

Filmmaker Shakti Samanta had said of the *Mahanayak*, 'Uttam was a very fine person. He was around 42 when he did *Amanush*. I was certain that only he could do justice to this complex role and he by far surpassed my expectations. I was sure that after *Amanush*, he would have made a place for himself in Hindi cinema, if only he had picked and chosen his roles with care. I had advised him to be selective. He was the reigning superstar of Bengal and didn't need to accept every Hindi film that came his way. He agreed with me, but an actress who influenced him believed differently. She thought he should make hay while the sun shone. The films he signed weren't worthy of him.'

In 1967, Uttam decided to take a gamble in Bollywood under his own production banner. He chose to remake his own hit film *Agnipariksha* in Hindi titled *Chhoti Si Mulaqat*, casting himself and Vyjayanthimala in the lead roles. In spite of a good storyline and good songs by

Mohammed Rafi like '*Chhoti Si Mulaqat Pyar Ban Gayi*' which became a hit, the film bombed at the box office. Uttam had pinned great hope on this film, and spared no expense to make it. *Chhoti Si Mulaqat* proved to be the worst debacle in his career. It almost ruined a man who had tasted immense success in Bengali films. He took a financial body-blow that badly affected his health.

Uttam's calibre as an actor in Bollywood was further established with two films, *Amanush* and *Anand Ashram.* Both were simultaneously made in Hindi and in Bengali, with Uttam in the lead in both versions. *Amanush* was directed by Shakti Samanta and the cast included Sharmila Tagore, Utpal Dutt and Asit Sen. It is the fascinating story of an alcoholic Madhusudan Roy Chowdhury (Uttam) in a village. The story traces the efforts of the police officer Bhuvan Sen to improve the village as well as probe the mysterious love life of the alcoholic with Lekha (Sharmila). The film was well received by both the national and Bengali film audience. It won the Filmfare award for Best Film and Uttam's work was well appreciated. Songs from this film became very popular, especially Kishore Kumar's '*Dil Aisa Kisine Mera Tora*', for which he received a Filmfare award. Uttam excelled in his lip sync, as always.

Anand Ashram, made by Shakti Samanta, was again a romantic film shot simultaneously in Hindi and Bengali, with Uttam and Sharmila in the lead roles. In *Anand Ashram,* Dr Deepak (Uttam), a doctor, has differences with his father (Ashok Kumar). He leaves his father's house when he marries Asha (Sharmila Tagore), who helps realise his dream of providing medical relief in rural areas. Uttam excels in the role of a husband who loses his wife in childbirth.

Dooriyan saw yet another Uttam and Sharmila Tagore pairing. The film was based on a storyline about marital problems in modern society, where an eventual separation affects the children. The parents finally decide to accord their children priority and brush aside their misunderstandings to make their children happy. Sharmila Tagore and Uttam gave brilliant performances in this family drama which portrays the sensitive parent-child relationship and the pain of separation for a family. The film also had some marvellous songs by Bhupinder like '*Zindagi Zindagi*' or '*Zindagi Me Jab Tumhare Gham Nahi The*'.

Of the four Hindi films Uttam worked in, he was romantically paired with Sharmila Tagore in three. Surprisingly, it was in these films that he achieved maximum success, despite their age difference. Sharmila's soft presence complemented Uttam's glamour in all the three films.

Choddobeshi (1971) was remade as *Chupke Chupke* (1975) by Hrishikesh Mukherjee and *Jeevan Mrityu* was remade in Hindi with the same name.

While shooting for Hindi films, Uttam used to good-naturedly grumble that Mumbai did not serve tea in earthen pots, something common in Kolkata even today.

Interestingly, despite the fact that Uttam could not work in many Hindi films, his talent as an actor par excellence was always recognised by the Hindi film industry. Son Gautam says he became aware of the immense respect his father commanded as an actor when they visited Mumbai for the premiere of Manmohan Desai's *Desh Premi* (1982). Apart from other Hindi film artistes, Gautam talked about the respect his father earned from the leading luminaries of Bollywood.

Amitabh Bachchan visited Uttam and touched his feet to seek his blessings and Rajesh Khanna visited him, too. It is reported that after seeing his work in *Chhoti Si Mulaqat*, the buzz in Mumbai was that, '*Ye to potential danger hai!*' (He is a potential danger). It is rumoured that some of the leading actors of those times were apprehensive about Uttam coming to Mumbai and the competition they may have to face from him. Around this time Uttam was offered yet another Hindi film *Avishkar* (1973), by Basu Bhattacharjee, but for some reason the superstar did not agree to do the film.

Both Uttam and Suchitra were glamorous personalities on the Bengali screen before they ventured into Hindi films. They found the world of Bengali films a trifle different from that of Hindi films. While glamour was of less significant for success in Bengali films where storyline, characterisation and acting took the lead, in Hindi films, it was, and still is, as important as acting.

Salil Dutta, who worked as an assistant to Bibhuti Laha, says he observed both Uttam and Suchitra closely during their shoots. After their individual forays into Hindi cinema, he observed that while Uttam maintained his previous persona, Suchitra had visibly changed, especially in her style of dressing.

Surprisingly, no Hindi filmmaker tried to utilise the screen chemistry Uttam and Suchitra shared. Had the two been paired in Hindi cinema, perhaps, they would have created as much a sensation in Bollywood as they did in Bengali cinema.

With Hindi films growing in stature to represent Indian cinema and Bengali cinema losing some of its sheen after the Uttam and Suchitra age, many Bengali actors forayed into Hindi films and tasted success in Bollywood: Rani Mukherjee, Kajol, Konkona Sen Sharma, Nandita Das, Bipasha Basu, Sushmita Sen, Rahul Bose and Raima Sen.

Apart from actors, Bengali directors often try their hand at Hindi cinema. Kolkata is a cultural melting pot and its influence on Hindi cinema is evident in films like Sudhir Mishra's *Calcutta Mail* (2003), Mani Ratnam's *Yuva* (2004), or Guru Dutt's *Sahib, Bibi Aur Ghulam*, with its horse-drawn carriages, fighting pigeons, palatial homes, and courtesans in 19th-century Kolkata, or even Sanjay Leela Bhansali's *Devdas* (2002) and Pradeep Sarkar's *Parineeta* (2005).

Kolkata of yore with its old-world charm lives on in Bollywood despite Uttam and Suchitra having faded from it.

9

Bollywood Romances

Is this true
That the earth can be wrapped in the end of my sari,
That my voice makes the world fall silent to hear me...

Rabindranath Tagore

On-screen couples have often contributed as much to making a film popular as script writers, music directors and directors put together. Ever since the emergence of mainstream cinema, the film industry has been dependent on these golden pairs that have lent charisma to the screen. It has been repeatedly proven that if there is no chemistry between the lead pair, the film is quickly forgotten.

Speaking of chemistry, American comedian and filmstar Groucho Marx once remarked, 'If actors don't fancy each other in real life, then it doesn't matter how good they are at acting. The sexual interaction just won't look good on film.'

Love blooming on the sets of films is common and has often resulted in many on-screen couples extending their love, off-screen. Pairs like Dharmendra-Hema Malini,

Rishi Kapoor-Neetu Singh and Amitabh Bachchan-Jaya Bhadhuri, have not only been lead pairs in reel life, they have also been very compatible couples in real life. In various polls about film icons that the youth remember in the country, few star pairs evoke memories of great romances of the past. For every *Dilwale Dulhaniya Le Jayenge* (1995) or *Kuch Kuch Hota Hai* (1988), there is a *Barsaat* (1949), *Kaagaz Ke Phool* (1959), *Mughal-e-Azam* (1960), *Pakeezah* (1972), or a *Bobby* (1973) that still strikes a sensitive chord. Such is the eternal appeal of these couples that neither changing times nor generational shifts can dull the sheen of these screen romances etched in public memory.

If chemistry is all about ego battles, sophisticated wordplay, sexual undercurrents or *double entendres*, what makes these couples lovable and legendary as on-screen pairs? Besides, what makes certain on-screen pairs click is a mystery with many answers—all partly true.

Filmmakers go to great lengths to ensure that the film draws out chemistry between the lead actors. After all, people feel happier to watch their own fantasies being recreated on screen. To bring about screen chemistry, earlier filmmakers often combined classic love stories with good scripts to produce popular films that the common man could relate to like *Mughal-e-Azam* and *Devdas*.

Ask any cinegoer about absolute romance and the scene cited would be that of Dilip Kumar and Madhubala in *Mughal-e-Azam*, where Salim caresses Anarkali with a feather. This scene will probably go down in the chronicles of Indian cinema as one of the most erotic scenes without the slightest hint of vulgarity in it, and is testimony to the fact that on-screen chemistry does not need sleaze or scantily dressed women to produce hit films. The recent crop of films including terrible remakes of Hollywood films, with their flashy extravaganza, over-exposed heroines and weak scripts have rightly left people craving for good old-fashioned romance.

Indian films, both regional and national, of the 1950s and 1960s, had original themes and saw some splendid film pairs depict romance. These pairs lent meaning and beauty to interesting scripts and a whole generation of viewers fell in love with them. An amazing thing about these pairs is that even without making a conscious effort to generate chemistry and passion on-screen, they sizzled. Their love scenes, chiefly expressed through symbolism, are also refreshingly different from the blatantly sexual and crude exploration of love portrayed today.

Screen chemistry is not totally dependent on personal relationships or the equations actors actually share with each other. Without physical proximity, old star pairs projected unbelievable passion. The use of sensual body language with ploys, such as discreet glances or the flirty flickering of the eyelashes was far more effective in setting the screen on fire.

Many may feel that a film can become an instant hit if the co-stars are romantically involved in real life. While this may be partially true, real-life couples have not always been successful in producing intense on-screen chemistry. Kareena-Saif, Ajay Devgn-Kajol and Abhishek Bachchan-Aishwarya Rai, some of the real-life couples of Indian cinema have proved beyond doubt that the opposite is actually true. Raj Babbar and Smita Patil, two popular stars of the 1980s who were involved with each other, signed several films together, but as fate would have it, most of these films did not do well at the box office, leaving producers struggling to recover their money. On the flipside, several producers have had to shelve their projects because the lead pair was no longer on good terms.

However, there are many instances of couples being successful off-screen, despite having their own private lives and spouses. Aamir Khan-Juhi Chawla, Anil Kapoor-Madhuri Dixit, Govinda-Karishma Kapoor, Shah Rukh Khan-Kajol and Hrithik Roshan-Aishwarya Rai are examples of such professionally successful on-screen couples.

Many stars who have been romantically linked with other heroes or heroines or have had successful hits with others have sometimes attained a special on-screen chemistry with just someone in particular. Raj Kapoor, who was a part of the famous Raj Kapoor-Nargis pair, was linked to other leading ladies like Vyjayanthimala and even Zeenat Aman. Strangely, people's fascination for his pairing with Nargis did not diminish over the years. In much the same way, the Madhubala-Dilip Kumar love story both on-screen and off-screen was legendary. Yet Dilip Kumar was extremely successful with his co-star Vyjayanthimala in several of their films together like *Naya Daur* (1957), *Madhumati* (1958), or *Sangharsh* (1968) Uttam and Suchitra, too, formed an everlasting pair in the eyes of Bengali cinema lovers. This in spite of the fact that Uttam was a married man involved with co-star Supriya Devi, and Suchitra was married, too.

Uttam was also successfully paired with Sabitri Chatterjee in about 27 films, many of which became hits. Sabitri has, in many interviews, spoken of her love for him. Uttam had also acknowledged that he was emotionally involved with her at one time. Yet till today, it is his chemistry with Suchitra that is still talked about.

Apart from Hindi cinema where celebrated star pairs created a sensation and dictated box-office hits and misses, Indian regional cinema has also seen successful screen couples who have contributed in their own way to the popularity of cinema of that region. In their togetherness, perfect timing and haunting screen presence, these couples wooed the audience into loving and idolising them. Examples, such as MGR-Jayalalitha in Tamil cinema and Raj Kumar-Leelavathi in Kannada cinema showcase the essence of celluloid togetherness that has influenced not just fans, but cinema in general.

When Uttam and Suchitra became a hit couple in Bengali cinema, there were several other star pairs in the national scene, notable because of their popularity, like Ashok Kumar-Devika Rani, Trilok Kapoor-Nirupa Roy and Raj Kapoor-Nargis. The glamour of Hindi films with sizzling star pairs successfully lured away a primarily Bengali audience. It was the Uttam and Suchitra combination that successfully stemmed the tide and brought back home a regional audience. Once this was accomplished, Uttam and Suchitra sustained their popularity despite the presence of better and glamorous actors in Hindi cinema.

The comfort level and space shared by two actors on-screen, their mental make-up and ability to relate to each other are some of the factors that make them good screen couples. In Indian cinema, some star combinations have had this rare privilege.

Raj Kapoor-Nargis

Probably the most memorable and the first-ever effective star pair in India, Raj Kapoor and Nargis inspired tremendous love and adulation. Both of them achieved great stardom as individuals and emerged as a much sought-after star pair. Amid rumours of their off-screen relationship, the star pair gave a series of hit films to cement a terrific bond on-screen, too. The couple starred in about 16 films together and projected an unabashed on-screen romance for almost eight years before they broke up.

Raj Kapoor met Nargis when he was barely 22. Trying to meet her mother Jaddan Bai, he ran into her daughter Nargis at their apartment. This first meeting was forever etched in Raj Kapoor's mind and he re-created it later in his film *Bobby*. A beautiful Nargis running a dirty hand across a lock of hair on her forehead was just the beginning of many more beautiful times together. Raj Kapoor is considered the greatest showman in Hindi cinema. He belonged to a film family—often called the first family of Hindi cinema—with the illustrious Prithviraj Kapoor as his father. He was an accomplished actor, director and producer. The winner of eight Filmfare Awards, his films *Awaara* (1951) and *Boot Polish* (1954) won international acclaim.

Nargis was a well-recognised actress and proved to be a lucky mascot for the RK banner, too. Her biggest triumph was in the role of Radha in *Mother India* (1957), for which she received an Academy Award nomination. The film also fetched her the award for Best Actress at the Karlovy Vary International Film Festival, and the Filmfare Award.

The chemistry of the Raj-Nargis pair was always electrifying and resulted in some of the greatest hits of the time including *Awaara, Shree 420* (1955), *Aag* (1948), *Andaz* (1949), *Barsaat* (1949) and *Chori Chori* (1956). Most of their films together have a classical touch, yet it is the unconcealed passion between the two that is astonishing. The pair was known as much for their sensuality as for their on-screen and off-screen passion. The Raj-Nargis on-screen pair was equally about soulful romances. Much of this chemistry came through in the beautiful songs picturised on them. Images of a wet and passionate Raj Kapoor and Nargis under one umbrella in '*Pyar Hua, Ikraar Hua*' from *Shree 420* is a celluloid fantasy even today. Again their '*Aaja Sanam Madhur Chandani Mein Hum*' from *Chori Chori* reminds us of their breezy yet, sensuous romance. In the most fitting tribute to this star pair, the famous RK banner bears the image of Nargis in passionate abandon in Raj Kapoor's arms.

Dev Anand-Suraiya

This star pair had the most romantic history, both in their reel and real lives. Suraiya and Dev Anand met on the sets of *Vidya* (1948). He was a new entrant to films, while she was already an established actress. While he became highly popular in his own right eventually, she saw unprecedented stardom, especially during 1948-49. The highest-paid female star during that time, Suraiya generated hysteria!

An incident, seemingly straight out of a film, brought them close. A suave and handsome Dev Anand saved a drowning Suraiya when their boat capsized during the shooting of *Vidya*. The couple worked in seven films together, of which *Vidya*, *Jeet* (1949), *Afsar* (1949), *Shair* (1949) were hits. The audience liked their pairing and news about their off-screen romance made their films more popular.

In an interview, Suraiya said, 'I worked with Dev in seven films. Inevitably, people started talking about our romance and my grandmother learnt of it. She was extremely angry because Dev was a Hindu and granny was very orthodox.' As their romance blossomed, gossip mills worked overtime within the industry and amid fans, too. Stories of how a romantic Dev Anand proposed to Suraiya at the Taj Mahal with a diamond ring kept doing the rounds. But the love story did not have a happy ending as Suraiya's grandmother, a staunch Muslim, opposed the relationship. Rumours have it that when she discovered the engagement ring, she threw it into the sea and threatened to have Dev Anand killed. The couple still met clandestinely with the help of friends like Durga Khote and Kamini Kaushal. Real-life drama ensued as Suraiya was supposedly told by her grandmother that their coming together would lead to Hindu-Muslim riots.

The besotted pair had planned to seal their love with marriage during a shooting sequence on the film sets. Dramatically, the sequence would be that of a marriage scene with the couple eloping, the only difference being that the marriage and eloping would be for real. Unfortunately, Suraiya's family came to know of it. Fearing for Dev's safety, she gave in to their demands, breaking Dev Anand's heart. Suraiya vowed never to marry and remained single all her life. Dev Anand married co-star Kalpana Karthik and went on to become one of the most popular heroes of Hindi cinema. Dev Anand's and Suraiya's films, apart from being hits, became popular for songs, such as '*Dil Ki Duniya Ujad Gayi*' and '*Kya Cheez Hai Muhabbat*' from *Shair*, and '*Layi Khushi Ki Duniya*' from *Vidya*.

Dilip Kumar-Madhubala

This was another passionate love affair in real life and on celluloid that gave rise to a charismatic on-screen pair in Indian cinema. Till today Madhubala is regarded as one of the most beautiful women in Hindi films, while Dilip Kumar, with his tremendous screen presence, was labelled the Tragedy King. Theirs was a pairing which had history and tragedy writ large on it. The Dilip Kumar-Madhubala affair, which was supposed to have begun on the sets of *Tarana* (1951), continued till the end of *Mughal-e-Azam* (1960) though many complications surfaced in the meantime. Their intensely passionate love story and eventual break-up itself could make a powerful screenplay. Incidentally, Madhubala's beauty was so mesmerising that many speak less of her acting capabilities. After a slew of films early in her career, Madhubala first made her impact in *Mahal* (1949) in the role of a gardener's daughter. Her dreamy looks struck a chord with the audience and her performance was well-received. The song '*Aayega Aanewala*' sung by Lata Mangeshkar further added to the popularity of the film. Madhubala had an innate sense of the comic in her, which was seen in one of her greatest hits *Chalti Ka Naam Gaadi* (1958), where she was paired with Ashok Kumar. The latter half of Madhubala's film career was replete with good films that showcased her talent. *Howrah Bridge* (1958), *Kaala Paani* (1958) and *Phagun* (1958) are some films that worked in her favour.

Dilip Kumar, on the other hand, is regarded by many as one of the greatest Indian actors. Having won the maximum number of Filmfare awards, he struck a balance between a variety of roles. His role in films, such as *Andaz, Aan* (1952), *Devdas, Azaad* (1955), *Mughal-e-Azam* or *Ganga Jamuna* (1961) showcased not only his potential as a great actor, but also his capability to handle and experiment with a wide range of roles.

Together, Dilip Kumar and Madhubala brought magic to the screen. Her innate sensuality and coquettish come-hither looks balanced with his sultry good looks created tremendous on-screen chemistry in *Tarana* (1951), *Sangdil* (1952) and Mehboob Khan's *Amar* (1953). In these three films, one witnesses their pairing in a different light from that in *Mughal-e-Azam.* Special mention must be made of *Tarana,* where romance started budding, with a palpable intimacy between the lead pair. Their pairing in *Mughal-e-Azam* created history. Madhubala as Anarkali looked beautiful, while Dilip Kumar as Prince Salim was grand in his mannerisms. In their romantic scenes together, they display heart-searing passion remembered even today.

The Dilip-Madhubala relationship lasted about eight years, through the making of *Mughal-e-Azam.* Towards the end of its filming (which took almost ten years), their relationship, which had seen many ups and downs, finally fizzled out. The biggest opposition to their relationship came from Madhubala's father Ataullah Khan who had total control over his daughter's life, including her money. Though he cited her young age and ill-health as impediments, it was probabaly the fear of foregoing the huge sums of money Madhubala was earning. Under the constant strain of parental opposition, the affair continued in a clandestine manner for some time, before it ended.

Playing Anarkali was an important landmark in Madhubala's career; it immortalised her in the hearts of millions. Scenes from the film showing Dilip Kumar looking passionately at her or stroking her cheeks and Madhubala with her mysterious smile are etched in the memory of audience, forever. While both stars worked with other co-stars, it is in their sublime togetherness that they are remembered even today as one of the finest star pairs of Hindi cinema. A public end to their love affair left Dilip Kumar very bitter and Madhubala broken and lonely, amidst ill health and a bad marriage with Kishore Kumar. Despite great popularity and audience clamouring to see them come together again, the couple never did, either in films or in life.

Guru Dutt-Waheeda Rehman

Waheeda Rehman and Guru Dutt formed an interesting pair that was not only popular but enriching, primarily due to their individual personalities. Guru Dutt was sensitive and poetic, a pioneer and a genius who was ahead of his times in many ways. Waheeda Rehman was a soft, dignified and classic beauty who touched everyone who encountered her. The Waheeda-Guru Dutt pair has mostly been about the pain and intensity of love rather than frolicking happiness. Guru Dutt was a big name in Hindi films, be that for his directorial ventures which earned him much critical and popular acclaim, or in front of the camera, as an actor. When the two met, Guru Dutt was already an established name while Waheeda Rehman was a struggling actress in the Telugu film industry. Guru Dutt introduced her to Hindi films and Waheeda was given roles that would establish her as an actress. She worked in *CID* (1956) with Guru Dutt where she played a negative character, which fetched her critical acclaim. In *Pyaasa*, she was a prostitute fascinated by the poetry of Vijay, played by Guru Dutt. *Pyaasa* was a landmark film that put the spotlight on Waheeda and earned both actors rave reviews. In both these films, the couple's chemistry was admired by their fans.

After *CID* and *Pyaasa,* the star pair worked as team and were associated with many projects together. Waheeda became Guru Dutt's favourite and the two were inseparable even as she joined his creative team. As a pair, they were successful in films including *Kaagaz Ke Phool, Kala Bazar* (1960), *Chaudhvin Ka Chand* (1960) and *Sahib Bibi Aur Ghulam.*

Many fans feel that the films of Guru Dutt and Waheeda Rehman were ahead of their times and the pair did not get the success that was rightfully theirs. The facial expressions of love and despair in the scenes where she is shown in the song '*Aaj Sajan Mohe Ang Laga Le*' with Guru Dutt made a tremendous impact. In a twist of fate, it was Geeta Dutt (Guru Dutt's wife) who sang for Waheeda as she romanced Geeta's husband in *Pyaasa.*

Waheeda and Guru Dutt worked together in *Kaagaz Ke Phool,* a poetic film that was probably not understood well by the audience of those times. The film was in many ways akin to Guru Dutt's life as it showed the story of a film director in love with his muse, ultimately alienated by his family. Not to be deterred by the failure of *Kaagaz Ke Phool,* Guru Dutt soon launched his next production *Chaudhvin Ka Chand,* a film that achieved great commercial success. Waheeda and Guru Dutt have never looked as good together as they did in this film. When Guru Dutt sang '*Chaudhvin Ka Chand Ho Ya Aftab Ho,*' the entire nation sang with him. Till today, the song and the film remain an epitome of romance in Hindi films.

Despite the fact that Guru Dutt was married to Geeta Dutt, he was smitten by the talented and good-looking Waheeda and the two were allegedly involved in a relationship. During the filming of *Chaudhvin Ka Chand,* it was rumoured that Waheeda had also responded to Guru Dutt's emotions, though she has maintained a stoic silence throughout. However, Geeta Dutt's knowledge of this romance proved to be an obstacle.

Meanwhile, Waheeda was confused and frustrated with the situation and set out to prove that she could be as good with other directors. She successfully worked in several hit films, such as *Bees Saal Baad* (1962), *Guide* (1965) and *Teesri Kasam* (1966). It is believed that Waheeda Rehman was under pressure while completing *Sahib Bibi Aur Ghulam.* Geeta Dutt made her displeasure known publicly by not singing for Waheeda in *Sahib Bibi Aur Ghulam.* Waheeda broke away from Guru Dutt soon after, both professionally and personally. The film was highly appreciated in India and won the President's Silver Medal, too.

Even though Guru Dutt's marriage to Geeta Dutt had turned shaky, he could not go back to a relationship with Waheeda. Thus ended a beautiful romance, which might have touched dizzying heights had it blossomed under the dual passions of films and love. It is said that Guru Dutt could not get over his lost love and committed suicide in 1964. Waheeda, on her part, married her co-star Kamaljeet.

The Waheeda-Guru Dutt pairing had more than just romance going for them. In their shared respect and admiration, they showcased something subtle yet refined, which was special.

Rajesh Khanna-Sharmila Tagore

Most cinephiles remember Rajesh Khanna as India's first superstar. He was a popular protagonist in many romantic, melodramatic and social films. He teamed up with Bengali beauty Sharmila Tagore to form one of the most sensuous and passionate couples in Indian cinema. Rajesh-Sharmila was a pair associated with down-to-earth, homely cinema that the audience could readily relate to. Though Rajesh Khanna worked in numerous films with Hema Malini and Mumtaz, he is most remembered for his romantic pairing with Sharmila Tagore. While both Rajesh Khanna and Sharmila Tagore were glamorous in their own way, Rajesh Khanna's romantic mannerisms and hype won him an extraordinary fan following.

In her own way, Sharmila Tagore was the glamour queen of her times, especially after her film *An Evening in Paris* (1967). Everything they did was mundane, yet scorching in its intensity. While Rajesh Khanna drove most females crazy with his sensuality, Sharmila's coy sexiness was alluring, making them a much loved couple. Together, they gave a string of musical hits. A song like '*Roop Tera Mastana*' from *Aradhana* (1969) embodies their full-blown screen romance and is remembered till date for the palpable sexual chemistry they exuded. In *Amar Prem*, one of the most popular films of this pair, a disillusioned Anand Babu (Rajesh Khanna) seeks solace in the company of a prostitute (Sharmila), without having a physical relationship with her. The film has many such endearing moments.

Songs account for a good deal of their chemistry in these films. When Anand Babu sings '*Chingari Koi Bhadke*' to Pushpa on a boat in *Amar Prem*, their love seems to transcend the physical to move on to the another level. Dialogues like '*Tumne to is kamre ko mandir bana diya*' (You have turned this room into a temple) as Anand babu addresses Pushpa, a prostitute, are romantically sublime. The two excelled in films like *Aradhana, Safar* (1970), *Amar Prem, Chhoti Bahu* (1971), *Avishkaar* (1973) and *Daag* (1973).

Dharmendra-Hema Malini

Hema Malini and Dharmendra are one of the most good-looking pairs of Hindi cinema. Their charming smiles and made-for-each-other expressions captured viewers' hearts. In the 1970s, the Hema-Dharmendra pair ruled the roost and was sought after by most producers. Hema and Dharmendra, lovingly known as 'Dream Girl' and 'Garam Dharam' respectively, hit it off both on-screen and off-screen and eventually got married. The two worked in numerous films together, starting with *Sharafat* (1970).

Most of their films owed their success to the popularity of their fabulous pairing. While Hema Malini represented eternal femininity with grace, shyness and immense beauty, Dharmendra was the epitome of masculinity with his rugged good looks and soft heart. Some of the films they worked in together were *Naya Zamana* (1971), *Raja Jaani* (1972), *Jugnu* (1973), *Sholay* (1975), *Seeta Aur Geeta* (1972), *Pratigya* (1975) and *Dil Ka Heera* (1979).

Hema and Dharmendra worked in close to 30 films, most of them hits. The Hema-Dharam magic was something that every viewer carried back home. They wooed millions, took away their gloom in darkened theatres, replacing it with sparkling new romance. While Dharmendra was the handsome and down-to-earth son of the soil, Hema was the exact opposite—the beautiful princess of Hindi cinema, haughty and unapproachable, always in control of herself. While Hema confessed to being attracted to his good looks, Dharmendra played the possessive lover by restricting other top heroes like Sanjeev Kumar and Jeetendra from wandering close to Hema. The lovers in real life eventually married in 1979, even though Dharmendra was a married man with children from his first marriage. The couple has two daughters, Esha and Ahana.

Their warm scenes in *Seeta Aur Geeta,* their couple act in *Sholay* or problematic situations in *Dil Ka Heera* speak of a terrific chemistry that was obvious in the most diverse roles. Added to this was the fact that both Hema and Dharmendra were popular actors in their own right, and their pairing proved to be a big box-office draw. Their act in *Sholay,* when Dharmendra as Veeru threatens to jump off a huge water tank to make her say 'Yes!' is remembered as one of their best performances together. Recently in a TV interview, Hema Malini admitted how she was smitten by a handsome Dharmendra and took the initiative in marrying him. Hema deserves credit for conducting her life with such dignity and discipline that few have been able to criticise her choices in life. Surprisingly, despite a very public affair and even marriage, the public never ostracised Dharmendra and Hema Malini, probably because the pair was so lovable that they were destined to be together!

Most couples discussed above have shared a close bond with each other. Perhaps, it is this bond that helped them understand each other so well and recreate history on the screen. In the case of Uttam and Suchitra, too, one can sense the magic. Irrespective of speculations about whether they had a real-life relationship or not, they shared a bond so delicate and precious that it seemed equally meaningful on-screen, too.

But what is it that distinguishes the Uttam and Suchitra pair? The answer calls for deep introspection on the common denominators in the films both worked in together. While every other Bollywood pair is usually identified with a particular side of love or emotion that they portray best, Uttam and Suchitra seemed to excel in all these shades and much more! The pair was as glamorous as Nargis-Raj Kapoor, in *Agnipariksha*, and as beautiful in their simplicity as Rajesh Khanna-Sharmila Tagore, in *Harano Sur*. The pathos of Guru Dutt and Waheeda Rehman is matched in films like *Sagarika* or *Shilpi*, and the spirited cheerfulness of the Dharmendra-Hema pair light up *Sare Chuattor* or *Saptapadi*. The list of films where Uttam and Suchitra remind us of our favourite Bollywood couple is long. And it is, perhaps, this bounty of varied togetherness that makes the Uttam and Suchitra combination a cut above the rest.

In their on-screen togetherness, the Bengali audience found not only Nargis-Raj Kapoor, but also Rajesh-Sharmila or a Dilip-Madhubala, all rolled into one! It is, perhaps, in the cherished smiles for each other, mutual passion, sustained love and capacity for pathos that Uttam and Suchitra reign supreme. This on-screen chemistry they shared has been imprinted on the hearts and minds of their fans. They have achieved the impossible—being spoken of in the same breath, unlike any other star pair of their age or in today's times!

While watching films today, one often misses such star performers and pairs who can carry the film on their own steam in contemporary cinema. Both in Bengali and Hindi films, star pairs that leave a lasting impression on the audience are rare. Performers, such as Debashree Roy, Prosenjit and Rituparna Sengupta in Bengali cinema might be highly recognised stars and good performers in their own right. Yet that magic, that instant charm that lit up the screen seems missing. In Hindi films, an Aamir Khan and Juhi Chawla, or a John Abraham and Bipasha Basu might have sparked passion in a single film, yet failed to sustain it in others.

In the good old days, a memorable lead pair, a good script and good music were all one needed to guarantee the success of a film. Opulence and splendour of the *Mughal-e-Azam* kind were rare. The smouldering chemistry between Raj Kapoor-Nargis, Rajesh Khanna-Mumtaz and Amitabh Bachchan-Rekha would create immense hysteria even around a low-budget film, adding enormously to their appeal and the consequent box-office potential.

Gulzar once said, 'A good love sequence is one where we can go beyond the body of the two people in love.' In this regard, couples of yore take the cake. In many cases of famous on-screen chemistry, star pairs didn't need to even touch each other to convey the depth of their romance. Yet they are still considered among the most engaging on-screen lovers that ever lived!

In today's world of fast food, fast films, fast link-ups and faster break-ups, where love letters have been replaced by greeting cards, and sweet nothings are sent off as SMS-s, popcorn romance has replaced the charm and grandeur of these magic pairs. However, a sizable chunk of today's audience, especially those in their 30s, understand and mourn the magic of such eternal leading pairs. Today's films are loud sex comedies, frivolous romances and constant experimentation in the presentation of violence. The very complexion of Hindi cinema has changed with time, with stylisation and props assuming more importance than casting and chemistry.

Contemporary filmmaker Rajkumar Santoshi, who has made memorable films like *Ghayal* (1990) and *Damini* (1993), feels that today's films mirror the attitude of the new generation towards life. About the chemistry between filmstars, he says, 'Unlike the past, today's stars treat films as a profession. The commercial aspect of business has overtaken the artistic aspect. In the olden days, filmstars poured their hearts into their roles. While doing a romantic scene, there were several instances where the heroine had actually fallen in love with the hero and *vice versa.* Today everything is treated with competence and clinical professionalism that takes away the magic of the moment. So the pairs have nothing to offer except technically correct performances.'

While what most star pairs of the older generation shared in a relationship may not have been love, it was certainly something enriching, which accounted for the craze they generated. In hindsight, it is obvious that in today's world, where passion is replaced by professionalism, it may take a long time to see a successful star pair as luminous as those that once were.

Epilogue: The Eternal Melody

When Uttam and Suchitra embraced each other or looked longingly at each other, their togetherness seemed to still time. Their wonderful on-screen unison, their smiles for each other in a world where they seemed to exist for the other, made one wish Uttam and Suchitra were as much a real-life couple in their perfect understanding of each other, as they were on celluloid. One could not but wonder if they ingeniously covered up their relationship or were in denial of something more intimate and personal.

Having researched many film journals, glossies and literature on both, it would be safe to conclude that what they had was so special that it was best kept away from the prying eyes of friends, colleagues and even the journalists of their times.

Though the paparazzi was not a force to reckon with those days, filmmakers feared the ire of 'Madam Sen'. Any report on the relationship, rumoured or true, would have had disastrous consequences for producers and filmmakers

In not divulging the truth, Uttam and Suchitra were, perhaps, bowing down to the social mores of their times. Perhaps, their relationship was so sacred that they made a conscious effort to keep it a secret. Or perhaps, there was no 'truth' to divulge.

Uttam and Suchitra continue to live in our hearts. In the end, that is all that matters.

Filmography

1953
Film: *Sare Chuattor*
Director: Nirmal De
Story: Bijon Bhattacharya
Screenplay: Nirmal Dey
Cinematographer: Amal Das, Nirmal Dey
Dialogue: Nirmal Dey
Music: Kalipada Sen
Lyricist: Sailen Roy

1954
Film: *Ora Thakey Odhare*
Director: Sukumar Dasgupta
Story: Premendra Mitra
Cinematographer: Banku Roy
Screenplay: Premendra Mitra
Dialogue: Premendra Mitra
Music: Kalipada Sen
Lyricist: Premendra Mitra

1954
Film: *Moroner Pore*
Director: Satish Dasgupta

Story: Ajit Mukhopadhyay
Cinematographer: Subodh Bandyopadhyay
Screenplay: Anil Dutta
Dialogue: Anil Dutta
Music: Sargam Unit
Lyricist: Mohini Chowdhury

1954
Film: *Sadanander Mela*
Director: Sukumar Dasgupta
Story: Moni Burma
Cinematographer: Banku Roy
Screenplay: Premendra Mitra
Dialogue: Premendra Mitra
Music: Kalipada Sen
Lyricist: Premendra Mitra

1954
Film: *Annapurnar Mandir*
Director: Naresh Mitra
Story: Nirupama Devi
Cinematographer: Bishu Chakraborty
Screenplay: Naresh Mitra
Dialogue: Naresh Mitra

1954
Film: *Agniparíksha*
Director: Agradoot(Bibhuti Laha)

Story: Ashapurna Devi
Cinematographer: Bijoy Ghosh, Bibhuti Laha
Screenplay: Nitai Bhattacharya
Dialogue: Nitai Bhattacharya
Music: Anupam Ghatak
Lyricist: Gauri Prasanna Majumdar

1954
Film: *Grihaprabesh*
Director: Ajoy Kar
Story: Kanai Basu
Screenplay: Tulsi Lahiri
Music: Mukul Roy

1955
Film: *Sanjher Pradeep*
Director: Sudhangshu Mukherjee
Story: Prabhabati Debi Saraswati
Cinematographer: Dibyendu Ghosh
Screenplay: Moni Burma
Dialogue: Moni Burma
Music: Manabendra Mukhopadhyay
Lyricist: Shyamal Gupta

1955
Film: *Sapmochan*
Director: Sudhir Mukherjee
Story: Falguni Mukhopadhyay

Cinematographer: Deojibhai Padhiar
Screenplay: Nripendrakrishna Chatterjee
Dialogue: Nripendrakrishna Chatterjee
Music: Hemanta Kumar Mukhopadhay
Lyricist: Bimal Chandra Ghosh

1955
Film: *Sobar Upore*
Director: Agradoot
Story: Nitai Bhattacharya
Cinematographer: Bibhuti Laha
Screenplay: Agradoot
Dialogue: Agradoot
Music: Robin Chatterjee
Lyricist: Gauri Prasanna Majumdar

(1956)
Film: *Sagarika*
Director: Agragami
Cinematographer: Bijoy Ghosh
Story: Nitai Bhattacharya
Music: Robin Chatterjee
Lyricist: Gauri Prasanna Majumdar, Pranab Ray, Nitai Bhattacharya
Screenplay: Agragami
Dialogue: Agragami

1956
Film: *Ekti Raat*
Director: Chitta Bose

Story: Balaichand Mukherjee(as Banophool)
Cinematographer: Bijoy Ghosh
Screenplay: Nripendrakrishna Chatterjee
Dialogue: Nripendrakrishna Chatterjee
Music: Anupam Ghatak
Lyricist: Gauri Prasanna Majumdar

1956
Film: *Trijama*
Director: Agradoot
Story: Subodh Ghosh
Cinematographer: Bibhuti Laha, Bijoy Ghosh
Screenplay: Subodh Ghosh, Nitai Bhattacharya, Agradoot
Dialogue: Subodh Ghosh
Music: Nachiketa Ghosh
Lyricist: Gauri Prasanna Majumdar

1956
Film: *Shilpi*
Director: Agragami
Cinematographer: Ramananda Sengupta
Story: Nitai Bhattacharya
Screenplay: Agragami
Dialogue: Agragami
Music: Robin Chatterjee
Lyricist: Pranab Ray

1957
Film: *Harano Sur*
Director: Ajoy Kar

Story: Nripendrakrishna Chatterjee
Cinematographer: Ajoy Kar
Screenplay: Nripendrakrishna Chatterjee
Dialogue: Nripendrakrishna Chatterjee
Music: Hemanta Kumar Mukhopadhay
Lyricist: Gauri Prasanna Majumdar

1957
Film: *Chandranath*
Director: Kartik Chatterjee
Story: Sharat Chandra Chattopadhyay
Cinematographer: Bibhuti Chakraborty
Screenplay: Nripendrakrishna Chatterjee
Dialogue: Nripendrakrishna Chatterjee
Music: Robin Chatterjee
Lyricist: Pranab Ray

1957
Film: *Pathe Holo Deri*
Director: Agradoot
Story: Pratibha Bose
Cinematographer: Bibhuti Laha
Screenplay: Agradoot
Dialogue: Agradoot
Music: Robin Chatterjee
Lyricist: Gauri Prasanna Majumdar

1957
Film: *Jiban Trishna*
Director: Asit Sen

Story: Ashutosh Mukherjee
Cinematographer: Anil Gupta
Screenplay: Asit Sen
Dialogue: Asit Sen
Music: Bhupen Hazarika
Lyrics: Pulak Bandopadhyay, Shyamal Gupta, Gauri Prasanna Majumdar

1958
Film: *Rajlashmi O Srikanto*
Director: Haridas Bhattacharjya
Story: Sharat Chandra Chattopadhyay
Cinematographer: GK Mehta
Screenplay: Haridas Bhattacharya
Dialogue: Haridas Bhattacharya
Music: Gyanprakash Ghosh
Lyrics: Shyamal Gupta, DM Mitholia

1958
Film: *Indrani*
Director: Niren Lahiri
Story: Achintya Kumar Sengupta
Screenplay: Nripendrakrishna Chatterjee
Dialogue: Nripendrakrishna Chatterjee
Cinematographer: Bishu Chakraborty
Music: Hemanta Kumar Mukhopadhay, Nachiketa Ghosh
Lyrics: Gauri Prasanna Majumdar, Satyendranath Dutta

1958
Film: *Surjo Toran*

Director: Agradoot
Story: Gauri Prasanna Majumdar
Cinematographer: Bibhuti Laha, Bijoy Ghosh
Music: Hemanta Kumar Mukhopadhay
Lyrics: Gauri Prasanna Majumdar

1959
Film: *Chawa Pawa*
Director: Jatrik
Story: Nripendrakrishna Chatterjee
Cinematographer: Anil Gupta
Screenplay: Nripendrakrishna Chatterjee
Dialogue: Nripendrakrishna Chatterjee
Music: Nachiketa Ghosh
Lyrics: Gauri Prasanna Majumdar, Shyamal Gupta

1961
Film: *Saptapadi*
Director: Ajoy Kar
Story: Tarashankar Bandopadhyay
Cinematographer: Ajoy Kar
Screenplay: Binoy Chattopadhyay
Dialogue: Binoy Chattopadhyay
Music: Hemanta Kumar Mukhopadhay
Lyrics: Gauri Prasanna Majumdar

1962
Film: *Bipasha*
Director: Agradoot
Story: Tarashankar Bandopadhyay

Cinematographer: Bibhuti Laha, Bijoy Bose
Screenplay: Gauri Prasanna Majumdar
Dialogue: Gauri Prasanna Majumdar
Music: Robin Chatterjee
Lyrics: Gauri Prasanna Majumdar

1967
Film: *Grihadaha*
Director: Subodh Mitra
Story: Sharat Chandra Chattopadhyay
Cinematographer: Anil Gupta, Jyoti Laha
Screenplay: Subodh Mitra
Dialogue: Subodh Mitra
Music: Rabindranath Tagore, Robin Chatterjee
Lyrics: Rabindranath Tagore, Pranab Ray

1969
Film: *Kamallata*
Director: Harisadhan Dasgupta
Story: Sharat Chandra Chattopadhyay
Cinematographer: Anil Gupta, Jyoti Laha
Screenplay: Harisadhan Dasgupta
Dialogue: Harisadhan Dasgupta
Music Director: Robin Chatterjee
Lyrics: Pranab Ray, Joydeb, Bidyapati, Chandidas

1971
Film: *Nabarag*
Director: Bijoy Bose
Story: Ashutosh Mukherjee

Cinematographer: Dilip Ranjan Mukherjee
Screenplay: Bijoy Bose
Dialogue: Bijoy Bose
Music: Hemanta Kumar Mukhopadhay, Rabindranath Tagore
Lyrics: Rabindranath Tagore

1972
Film: *Alo Amar Alo*
Director: Pinaki Mukherjee
Story: Pratibha Bose
Cinematographer: Anil Gupta, Jyoti Laha
Screenplay: Pinaki Mukherjee
Dialogue: Pinaki Mukherjee
Music: Pabitra Chattopadhyay
Lyrics: Pulak Bandopadhyay, Rabindranath Tagore

1972
Film: *Har Mana Har*
Director: Salil Sen
Story: Tarashankar Bandopadhyay
Cinematographer: Anil Gupta, Jyoti Laha
Screenplay: Salil Sen
Dialogue: Salil Sen
Music: Sudhin Dasgupta
Lyrics: Pulak Bandopadhyay, Sudhin Dasgupta

1975
Film: *Priyo Bandhobi*
Director: Hiren Nag

Story: Prabodh Kumar Sanyal
Cinematographer: Kanai Dey
Screenplay: Hiren Nag
Dialogue: Hiren Nag
Music: Nachiketa Ghosh
Lyrics: Gauri Prasanna Majumdar

Acknowledgements

The process of setting about thanking people who have been with me while writing this book is a rather humbling one, simply because their contributions in matters ranging from encouragement, advice and support is beyond words. Nevertheless, this space does merit some significant names without whose support the book would truly have been rudderless.

The enormity and the love of Uttam and Suchitra's influence on me would have remained within had it not been for my family and friends and their unconditional support in so many ways.

I take this opportunity to also extend my gratitude to my friend and well-wisher SMM Ausaja who extended help in collecting visuals for the book, to the staff of the National Library Kolkata, the staff of National Film Archive of India (Pune), the staff of Satyajit Ray Film and Television Institute and my publisher, Ajay Mago. I am also grateful to Mr Gopal Krishna Roy for his love and valuable time, Smt Shoma A Chatterji for her encouragement and Mr Rudrajeet Mukherjee for the photographs, used in this book.

For the many musings, both big and small, to the man on the road or an Uttam and Suchitra crazy Kolkata, I remain indebted.

Acknowledgements